Jade's scent hit him. It was just like he'd remembered—a floral aroma. Pleasant. Nixon's stomach rumbled. Was he hungry—or was that reaction triggered by the memory of her scent? Quickly, he poured a cup of black coffee and returned to his spot with his bagel and a small serving of cream cheese. Tearing his focus away from her, he dived in on his bagel. She came and sat next to him. The tent card in front of her read Jade Chandler.

Jade Chandler. Nixon spoke the name in his head with warning. Politely, she nodded and said a cool "Good morning," as if she could have heard him.

"Good morning." He held his hand out. "Nixon Gaines."

She had a strong handshake and her touch made that sensation rise up on his skin again.

"Nice to meet you." She turned her attention to the coffee and croissant in front of her.

"Jade Chandler, huh?" Nixon lifted a brow and nodded. He had repeated her name just to taste it on his lips.

His mother had cautioned him about women who had a certain effect on men. Their lure was like the sticky silk of a spider's web. Nixon couldn't ~~pull~~ his attention away for⬚⬚⬚⬚⬚⬚⬚⬚⬚⬚⬚⬚⬚⬚ man in him. Only m⬚⬚⬚⬚⬚⬚⬚⬚⬚⬚⬚⬚⬚⬚ it and wanted⬚⬚⬚⬚⬚⬚⬚⬚⬚⬚⬚⬚⬚⬚⬚⬚s

Dear Reader,

I'm excited for you to experience the youngest sister in the Chandler clan's story. Meet Jade and her amazing hero, Nixon Gaines. They never intended to mix business with pleasure but couldn't seem to help themselves. There was no way they could deny the electrifying chemistry between them. A few things threatened to keep them from connecting—first a simple misunderstanding about Nixon's intentions and then…an old friend of Jade's. Will these issues get in the way of the best love both Jade and Nixon have ever experienced? Enjoy finding out and when you're done, send me a message. I'd love to hear from you.

Ciao,

Nicki

Diamonds FOR THE Holidays

NICKI NIGHT

H HARLEQUIN® KIMANI™ ROMANCE

Recycling programs
for this product may
not exist in your area.

ISBN-13: 978-1-335-21693-9

33614080853418

Diamonds for the Holidays

HARLEQUIN®
www.Harlequin.com

Printed in U.S.A.

Nicki Night is an edgy hopeless romantic who enjoys creating stories of love and new possibilities. Nicki has a penchant for adventure and is currently working on penning her next romantic escapade. Nicki resides in the city that dreams are made of, but occasionally travels to her treasured seaside hideaway to write in seclusion. She enjoys hearing from readers and can be contacted on Facebook, through her website at nickinight.com or via email at NickiNightwrites@gmail.com.

Books by Nicki Night

Harlequin Kimani Romance

Her Chance at Love
His Love Lesson
Riding into Love
It Started in Paradise
Desire in a Kiss
It Must Be Love

This book is dedicated to my current hero
and biggest cheerleader, Mr. Big Les.

Acknowledgments

With God anything is possible.
Diamonds for the Holidays is my seventh romance title
and the fourth book in the Chandler Legacy series.
I'm more grateful for this journey than words
can express. To God be the glory.

Harlequin Kimani fulfilled my publishing dreams.
Thanks to my editor, Glenda Howard, for your
great ideas and patience! To Sara Camilli,
thanks for always having my literary back.

I'm so thankful to my family for lending me to
my passion over and over again and not considering it
any kind of robbery. Team Flagler is the best!

To my literary sisters, you keep me inspired,
laughing, empowered and off the ceiling! Thank you
Beverly Jenkins, Brenda Jackson, Zuri Day,
Tiffany L. Warren, ReShonda Tate Billingsley,
Victoria Christopher Murray, Elle Wright,
Sheryl Lister, Sherelle Green, AD and so many more.

To my street team, I appreciate you more than you
can comprehend. Priscilla Johnson, Rowena Winfrey,
Michelle Chavis, Shavonna Futrell, Shannon Harper,
Cheryl McClinton, Deirdre Young and
Yolanda Rigby, you ladies are the bomb diggity!

Chapter 1

Jade spotted him right away. Her heart rate quickened and she could feel the rapid thump in her chest—a prominent thud that made her think the other folks at her table might hear it, too. Despite applying her best effort to keep her eyes on the gentleman she was meeting with, she fought hard against her will to avoid looking back at her ex, sitting at the table with a beautiful woman. She smiled at the executive director across from her, who was speaking so passionately about his nonprofit organization that served families of his community.

Jade was interested in what he was saying. She truly was, and had even called the meeting herself. But now, with Mitch Davidson seated just a few feet away from her, all she could think about was how she'd messed up and lost him for good. How could she let that perfect man escape her flighty grasp? Was that woman he sat with his new fiancée or was he entertaining business peers, like her? Jade nodded, agreeing to the bit she'd clearly heard from the man in front of her. The eloquent way he described his mission and vision was falling on filtered ears. Watching Mitch as she was, most of what she now heard sounded more like incoherent rambling. A few words here and there came through with clarity.

Hopefully, Mitch hadn't seen her. There would be a possibility that she could get out of the restaurant undetected. Jade politely excused herself and headed to the ladies' room.

"Get it together, Jade." She scolded her reflection. "You've been over him for a while now." *Right?*

A toilet flushed and a petite woman stepped out of the stall. She raised her brows at Jade in the mirror, connecting, letting her know without words that she understood. Jade smiled back and waited for the woman to exit. When the door clicked shut, she sighed.

Why was she reacting this way? They'd parted ways almost a year ago. Jade shook her head. The answer was clear. It was one thing to know he had moved on, but to see him at that restaurant—which used to be one of their favorite places—with another woman made everything more real. If this beauty was the new lucky woman, she truly had a prize. One that Jade failed to appreciate until after she'd tossed him away. And why? Because commitment frightened her—that was why.

"Okay, lady! You've got business to handle." She washed her hands, stuck them under the forceful hand dryer and headed to her table.

On the way back, she noticed that Mitch was gone. Relief paraded through her core. Before getting too excited, she looked around the restaurant to make sure he wasn't there. Just beyond the front door, she saw him, tall, handsome, and holding the woman's hand. They kissed—a soft slow peck—one that clearly laid claim to the other. He let his free hand slip over her backside. The woman giggled. They released their grasp, the gesture slow and hesitant. They didn't want to let each other go. Even from inside, Jade could spot the ring on her finger. Jade shook her head and, with one last sigh, let it all go.

At the table, Jade tried her best to give her full attention to the gentleman she was meeting with, and relished the excitement in his eyes when she invited him to submit a proposal for funding before ending their meeting. Inside her car, she dialed her cousin Kendall. To the world, Kendall was a famous pop artist. But to Jade she was her closest friend ever since the days of playing dress-up in their mothers' closets.

"Hey, Jade."

"I just saw him…and her."

"Who? Oh no!" Kendall's gasp was airy. "Him!" she sang. "And his fiancée?"

"Yep." Jade took a deep breath and dropped her head back on the headrest.

"Are you okay?"

"I'm fine. I thought I heard he was engaged, but seeing them together made it so…real."

"Did you say anything to him?"

"No. I'm not sure if he even saw me." What if he had?

"Do you still love him?"

Jade paused a moment. "I don't think so." She was as honest as she could be.

Silence hung between them for several moments.

"I wonder if he did see you, but didn't say anything because he was with her," Kendall finally said.

"Yeah." Old feelings bubbled to the surface. Jade wondered if the fiancée was giving him the things she couldn't. "Anyway," she huffed, "that's in the past now."

"Yes. It. Is! Why don't you come see me? We can do a long weekend on Catalina Island. Meet some gorgeous men and get your mind off of him. It's time for you to really move on and find someone new."

"Humph."

"Don't sound so glum. I just said 'meet' some gorgeous men, not bring them home to meet our mothers and get married." Kendall's laugh poured through the phone and Jade pictured her bent forward, slapping her thigh the way she always did. "Let loose a little—know what I mean?"

"Hey," Jade prompted when their laughter died down, "have you thought about settling down?"

Silence ensued, saying more than words could offer. "No time soon," Kendall finally said. "Let history tell it and that answer may change to never. The public can be cruel."

"I can imagine," Jade said, without rehashing the viral debacle Kendall's last breakup had become.

"What about your visit?" Jade perfectly understood Kendall's timely change of subject. Their conversation was moving toward a heavy matter. "Check your calendar and see when you can come. I'll send you my new tour dates and we can work around those. Why don't you come to one of my shows? I could use a good dose of normal."

"Yeah! And I could use a vacation."

Kendall squealed. "Good. I haven't seen you since Chloe's wedding. I gotta run now, but call me later and we'll work it out. Okay?"

"Okay, Ken."

"And don't sit around wondering 'what if.' Maybe things didn't work out between the two of you because there was another amazing man coming your way."

"You, too." Jade chuckled. "Talk to you later, Ken." Before she could think about meeting other men, she had to make sure she got Mitch all the way out of her system.

Chapter 2

"Mr. Gaines." Alex Brentworth greeted Nixon with a firm handshake. "Please." He waved toward the chair in front of his massive mahogany desk. "Have a seat."

Nixon stood tall, tugged on his tailor-made suit jacket and sat down. With his back firmly pressed against the tufted burgundy leather chair, he crossed his legs and flashed a proud grin. "Always a pleasure, Mr. Brentworth."

Alex chuckled. "Enough with the formalities, Nixon." He sat back and chewed on the end of an unlit cigar. "Congratulations! I hear you're quite the negotiator lately."

Nixon smiled again. "That's what they say."

"It certainly is." Alex studied Nixon for a moment. Alex's smooth mannerisms reminded Nixon of the polished and savvy Wall Street kind of man he'd seen in movies. "It most certainly is," Alex repeated. "A few of us are getting together for dinner tonight. How about you join us?"

Nixon kept his composure. "Thanks for the invitation. Let me check my calendar." He pulled his cell phone from the clip on his belt buckle. Even if he had plans, he wasn't going to turn down a dinner with the company's top execs. Sure enough, he was supposed to meet a friend for dinner. "All clear. What time should I meet you?"

"Seven thirty at Manning's…on Northern."

"Anytime is a good time for a great steak."

"You've got that right. I'm glad you're able to join us tonight. I think you'll find the conversation quite interesting."

Nixon's curiosity was piqued. Alex was a strategic guy who did nothing without an agenda. Nixon sat for a silent moment. Several questions crossed his mind. Not wanting to appear anxious, he didn't let those inquiries pass his lips. He stood and righted his jacket.

"Looking forward to it, Alex. I'm sure it will be a great time."

"So am I." Alex nodded. "So am I," he repeated in his assured way.

What was Alex up to? He was an old-school executive who preferred face-to-face interactions. "You can't read people in an email," he'd once told Nixon. But Nixon couldn't read Alex, either. Something was up and Nixon couldn't wait to get to dinner and find out what it was.

For the first time in weeks, Nixon left work on time. At home, he showered and pulled one of his best suits from the closet, a stylish navy blue number that he usually reserved for special occasions. Nothing less would be suitable for dinner with his company's senior executives in one of the most upscale steak houses on Long Island. There would be nothing casual about this environment.

Nixon arrived a few minutes early, but handed his keys over to the valet only after spotting two of the executives entering the restaurant. From the doorway, the dimly lit space offered an air of posh living. Nixon was greeted by a polished-looking host with salt-and-pepper hair, wearing a black suit. He led him to his table. The murmur of jazz music and the rumble of blended voices filled the place, which was packed for a Wednesday night. Nixon assumed that most of these well-dressed patrons, like him, were more likely to be talking business and making deals rather than sharing generic, casual conversations.

When he arrived at the table, Alex and the other two men—Jeff, the CEO, and Benjamin, the VP of Mergers and Acquisitions—stood. Alex was the president of that division. Nixon cleared his throat before greeting each with a firm handshake.

"Glad you could join us." Jeff nodded as he returned to his seat.

"Good to see you." Benjamin patted Nixon's shoulder.

Alex gestured to an approaching waiter, and moments later he returned, setting in front of each of them a glass half filled with what Nixon assumed was one of the finest single malt scotches a high-end restaurant could obtain. One shot of some of those luxurious libations could cost over half his rent. The waiter took their orders and together the gentlemen clinked glasses in a quick toast.

"How's life treating you outside of work?" Jeff asked him.

"Well, I must say. No complaints here."

"Good."

"And you?" Nixon made direct eye contact with each of them.

They shared a few more moments of cordial conversation, getting all the pleasantries out of the way. Nixon engaged as expected, but longed to get to the purpose of their invitation.

Alex took another sip, pressed his lips in appreciation of his drink and held his glass in the air. "Exquisite. Great choice, Benjamin." Placing his glass on the table, he looked over at Nixon. "I guess you're wondering why we invited you to join us tonight."

Nixon felt like Alex read his thoughts. "I am a little curious, of course." He felt more anxious in that moment. To calm his nerves, Nixon sipped and sat back, hoping to exude confidence as opposed to nervousness.

"Well." Alex leaned forward. "Let's get right to the point."

"We like what we've seen from you," Jeff said.

"And we have something for you to consider," Benjamin added.

The three of them spoke a well-choreographed dance of intrigue. Each picked up where the other left off, without a stutter.

"We have no promises to make," Alex said.

"However, we know what you're capable of," Jeff started.

"And have seen the accomplishments accredited to you in business development," Benjamin added.

"The bottom line is we see a future for you in Mergers and Acquisitions. The potential is great and the money is potentially limitless. It's the side of the business where the strong thrive, and your keen negotiation skills could be put to good use," Alex said.

The three of them sat back, eyes trained on Nixon, lips pressed together. They peered silently—in sync. Waiting.

At first Nixon nodded knowingly. He was being sized up. In the timeliest of fashions, the mature waiter arrived with their orders. He placed a choice cut of chateaubriand before Nixon and sides of sautéed spinach and garlic potatoes. The waiter bowed before departing, leaving Nixon to the three men peering back at him.

He cleared his throat again. "I'm grateful that you would consider me. I do enjoy my work and being with Wakeman Foods." Nixon nodded at the CEO. "I haven't studied much of the mergers and acquisitions arena."

"If…" Alex paused and sipped from his glass. "…an opportunity should avail itself, I assure you you'll be trained by the best in the business."

"On that note, we have another opportunity for you," Benjamin said.

Nixon raised his brows.

"There's an executive leadership fellowship that's about to launch here on Long Island. Wakeman Foods invested in the program. That secured us a spot so that one of our employees could participate. It could prove to be a great opportunity, since you're a fairly new Long Island professional. And it will raise your profile as an emerging executive and expand your network. An all-around win, regardless of what your future endeavors may be," Alex said, raising an eyebrow in turn.

"Now, you don't have to answer us this evening. We want you to think about it," Jeff said.

"Just know that you have our support in whatever you decide. It's an impressive program. One that many of the best business minds have emerged from, and they finally brought it here to Long Island." Benjamin's comments sealed Nixon's decision.

There was no way Nixon would turn down that offer. Coming from modest means as he had, whether he moved over to mergers and acquisitions or not, the program could benefit his career in countless ways.

Before Nixon could respond, which would have been

an immediate but anxious "yes," Jeff chimed in. "For now, enjoy your meal."

And just like that, the conversation was over. They ate their pricey steaks and seamlessly switched to non-work-related topics. Jovial tales of trysts on the golf course, in travel, sailing and a bunch of other things became part of the dialogue. Nixon engaged, but couldn't keep his mind off the possibilities they'd presented during dinner. His professional future had just brightened beyond his expectations. That would certainly make his father proud—hopefully.

Chapter 3

"Whew!" Jade plopped into her seat at the diner. "Ann, thanks so much for meeting with me this morning."

Ann dismissed Jade's gratitude with a wave. Her bloodred nails made her slender fingers look longer. Ann sat back in her seat. With one finger, she swiped the long hair hanging over one eye out of the way. Her fluid, tender mannerisms and refined stature gave her the grace of a mature model. Yet as a businesswoman she was steadfast and firm. "It's no trouble at all," she said. "In fact, it's my pleasure. You know how much you and your parents mean to me."

Jade sighed. Her shoulders lowered.

"What's wrong, dear? Was it something I said?" Ann gently rested her hand over Jade's. The large diamond on her ring finger caught the light and gleamed with a radiant sparkle. Despite her husband's passing several years before, Ann still wore her engagement ring and wedding band every day.

"No. Not exactly."

Ann tilted her head inquisitively and Jade groaned. "I love my parents," she continued. "I know firsthand how amazing they are, but I need to make a name for myself. I feel like I'm always in their shadow." A few moments of silence fell between them. "I'm sorry. That's not why we're here. Let's just drop it."

"Oh." Ann wagged her finger with vigor. "We're definitely not dropping this. Waiter!" She turned toward the lanky young man passing their table. "We'll need two cups of strong black coffee, please." Ann turned back to Jade. "Come on. Talk to me. I wouldn't be worth a damn as a mentor if I let something that bothers you this much slide by."

Over coffee and croissants, Jade explained how she'd been feeling about her professional life. "I just can't get out from under them. I want to be respected for what I'm capable of bringing to the table."

Ann sat quietly. At one point Jade wasn't sure she was listening, but when she looked up into her caring eyes she could tell that Ann had taken in every word.

"I don't know what to do. And then…sometimes I feel guilty." Instinctively, Jade averted her gaze to the knife she'd just used to butter her croissant—as if a croissant needed more butter.

Ann just smiled. Jade waited for her to say something, and when she kept quiet, Jade felt compelled to continue speaking.

"I guess it's part of 'paying my dues.'" She fell silent again.

Ann put her hand over Jade's again. "You're right."

Shocked, Jade looked Ann straight in the eyes. "I'm right?"

"Yep. It's time people get to know the brilliant, dynamic professional that is Jade Chandler." Ann gestured as if she were announcing Jade's presence.

"I'm right?" Jade repeated. Her brows creased in confusion. She shook her head. "It feels...selfish."

"There's nothing selfish about it. It's time for you to spread your professional wings."

A smile eased across Jade's face. Ann's simple words penetrated her soul. That was exactly what she'd been wanting. This was why she loved Ann. Ann understood her.

"But I don't want to leave the company."

"And you don't have to. You just need to put your stamp on it...develop your own legacy."

Jade nodded slowly as Ann's words sank in. "I don't know if Mom would like that." Jade may have been the executive director of the Chandler Foundation, but El basically ran it from her perch at Chandler's restaurant.

Ann reared her head back. "I'd be surprised if she wasn't expecting it at some point. Chairwoman or not, she wants the foundation to be successful, just like you do." Ann rested her elbow on the table and pointed at Jade. Jade straightened her back, as the gesture seemed like a reprimand. "The road to success is not just paved with El's ideas. They—" she waved her hand, referred to the board "—govern the company. You, my dear, run the company. It's the day-to-day that truly makes it successful."

In that moment, Jade felt so empowered. It was like a light switched on in her head. Immediately, she knew what she had to do. Now she just needed to find a way to make it happen.

"As a matter of fact..." Ann's words drew attention back to their conversation. "...there's an opportunity coming up that I think might be good for you." Ann pulled out her phone. "Give me one second."

Ann dialed a number, lifted her refined chin and waited for the person to answer. Jade could hear the ringing from her side of the table and wondered who she'd called. Like her mother and father, Ann was extremely well connected and practically a legend in the nonprofit sector. She'd spent decades running organizations and serving on boards, and now she simply consulted. More than Jade's own parents, Ann had taught her everything she knew about running the foundation. Her mom and dad were businesspeople, and running a nonprofit organization was a totally different experience than running a corporation.

"Tony…" Ann stretched his name into a melody. "Yes! I know…It's been a while…How are Shelly and the kids?" She looked over at Jade and winked as she continued her call. "That's just wonderful. Tell her I said hello and kiss the kids for me, will you? Listen, are you still working with that leadership program? Oh…Really?" Ann's brows creased and Jade wished she could hear more than a muffled voice. She wanted to know what this Tony guy was saying. "I see…You do that and get right back to me, okay? I appreciate it…I'll be waiting…You, too, darling. Take care."

"What happened?" Jade blurted the second Ann tapped the end button. She had no clue what the call was about but she was curious just the same.

"Consider yourself in."

"In what?" Jade looked at Ann skeptically.

Ann chuckled. "The Executive Leadership Program."

Jade leaned over the table to get closer. "Wait—that national program?"

"That's the one."

"Won't I have to go into the city?"

"No. They're bringing the program to Long Island. Isn't that wonderful?" Ann clasped her hands together.

"But isn't that super hard to get into?"

Ann tilted her head sideways and pursed her lips. Apparently she had momentarily forgotten who she was dealing with.

"You don't worry about that, dear. Tony will handle everything."

Jade sat back. Suddenly she felt giddy. "You really think you can get me in?"

"It's already done."

"Wow!" Jade was impressed. "That's what Tony said?"

"No."

"No?" Jade was confused again.

"But don't you worry. You will get in."

Ann's phone rang. She tapped the phone icon. "Hello… Wonderful. I knew I could count on you…I'll text you her email address so you can send the documentation over right away…Monday? Okay. Enjoy your day, dear." Ann set her phone down and cast a proud smile in Jade's direction. "This is going to be wonderful. You're going to gain quite a bit of recognition after this. Not to mention the great network that you're about to be open to. You'll be matched with professionals who have already graduated from the program. They make great mentors."

"Thank you so much, Ann. I understand that some pretty prominent professionals went through this program. I'm excited."

"People will come to know you for the dynamic professional that you are."

"It's about time!" Jade cackled. The sound of her laugh nearly hit the rafters. A few customers inside the diner looked their way. Ann shook her head and laughed, too.

Jade's day had been turned around just that fast. She no longer felt down. And although she knew little about what happened in the program, she did know what happened to professionals once they had come through it. Many of them hit the fast track to professional stardom, being recognized as "ones to watch" and topping lists of rising professionals in the media. This would be great for the foundation, but most important, it would truly set her apart as an executive and carve out her own space as a professional.

Jade felt giddy. She couldn't stop herself from smiling and didn't want to leave Ann just yet. "How about another cup?" Jade lifted her coffee mug and gazed at her appealingly.

"Oh, why not?" Ann shrugged. "Waiter!"

Their conversation was lighter now. Jade sat back easily. The tension she'd carried in her shoulders when she arrived had dissipated. She and Ann talked about anything and everything. When Ann slipped into her more colorful vernacular, it made Jade laugh hard. Her authenticity intrigued Jade. She could see herself maturing into a mixed version of Ann, her mother and her aunt Ava Rae. They were all so different, yet so smart, strong and unapologetically womanly.

Around them the diner seemed to have gotten busier. Almost every seat and booth was filled. Waiters and the hostess moved about swiftly. A deep voice rumbled through the diner and Jade froze. The smile fell from her lips. She knew that voice, but refused to turn around.

"Right over here is fine." It was that voice again.

"Jade. Darling. Are you okay?"

Ann had noticed. She didn't want her to. Jade fumbled for a second. "Oh…me." She let out a nervous laugh. "I'm fine. I just remembered something that I had to do."

Ann looked at her watch. "Well, the morning is almost over. You probably need to get back to the office." She placed her hand over Jade's again. "This was great.

I always enjoy our meet-ups. You go ahead. I'll take care of the bill."

"Are you sure?"

Ann dismissed her inquiry with a wave. "Oh please. I know I'm retired, but I did pretty well for myself while I worked. I should be able to cover coffee and croissants," she teased.

"Okay." Jade got up from her seat, leaned over and gave Ann a tight hug and a kiss. "Thanks so much."

Jade could still hear that voice. It didn't blend with the other voices in the diner. His, she heard above the rest. She hadn't seen Mitch, but knew he was there— most likely seated somewhere near her and Ann. Trying to pinpoint his proximity, Jade attempted to walk away from the sound of him, but instead ended up going right past his booth.

"Jade? Is that you?"

Jade halted midstep.

"Jade!"

She contemplated acting as if she hadn't heard him, but knew that wouldn't fly. Jade turned slowly, threw a cheery smile on her face and feigned surprise. "Mitch?" She furrowed her brows.

"Yeah!" He stood and stepped toward her with open arms.

She felt her body tighten. His embrace surrounded her before she could protest.

"It's so good to see you. How long has it been?"

Not long enough! "It's been a while."

If she thought about it, she could probably calculate the time down to the number of months, weeks, days and hours since she'd told him that she didn't want to be with him anymore. They wanted different things out of life, she'd told him. He wanted commitment, a marriage and a family. Jade couldn't see any of that happening anytime soon. Months had passed and he'd moved on by the time she realized that what she really wanted was him. Jade had let a good thing slip from her grasp.

The next thing she'd known, friends reported spotting him with another woman. Soon after that she'd heard rumors of him being engaged. Fortunately, she hadn't personally witnessed any of this, for months, until the other week when she was at the restaurant with that potential grantee. Everything she felt had come crashing back, but it was too late. Jade wasn't one to fawn over any man too eagerly, but she knew she'd made a grave mistake letting this one go.

"How's the family?" Mitch's question pulled her from her thoughts.

"Oh. They're fine." She shrugged. On the outside, she hoped a cucumber couldn't rival her coolness. Inside, air swirled in her chest.

"That's good to hear." The two of them stood for a few silent, awkward moments. Mitch's eyes locked on hers. She turned away slightly and raised her brows. She wanted to ask him about his fiancée, but refused to let that curiosity pass her lips. Confirmation of those rumors would have been nice.

"Oh!" Mitch tapped his forehead. "How rude of me. Sorry. Paul, this is…an old…friend of mine, Jade." Mitch paused again; the silence between his words spoke volumes. At least to Jade. "Chandler. Jade Chandler." He repeated her name in the correct formation and then turned to Jade. "Paul is a friend and client."

Jade didn't miss the pauses in Mitch's introduction. He'd never been one to stutter.

Paul stood and extended his hand. "Nice to meet you."

"It's nice to meet you, too." She turned to Mitch. "It

was really nice seeing you, but I'd better get going." Turning slightly back toward Paul, she said, "Have a good day."

Jade turned on her heels and left. She didn't want to read too much into the pauses when Mitch spoke. She noticed them, but wasn't sure if it was her being nostalgic or hopeful.

When she reached the office, the scent of Mitch still lingered on her. She remembered how it had gotten there. His embrace. Mitch had always given the best hugs.

Chapter 4

Nixon hadn't seen his mother in several weeks. They spoke every single day, but that was nothing like seeing Gloria's beautiful brown skin, the color of cardboard, or smelling the sweet scent of her signature floral perfume that lingered long after her hugs. The anticipation of being squeezed in her loving embrace even made the Bronx traffic bearable. Summer was near its end and there was a hint of fall crispness in the air. Nixon opened the windows and let the fresh autumn-like air rush against his smiling face. Matching the drumbeats flowing from the car radio, Nixon tapped the same tempo on his steering wheel with his fingers and thumbs.

Work had kept Nixon more than busy. Those long hours spilled over into his weekends. Between new strategies for business development and the steady pull from the execs in Mergers and Acquisitions, Nixon felt like he'd been running on a hamster wheel. He looked forward to starting the Executive Leadership Program, knowing that in a few months they would have to travel to sunny Southern California to meet up with execs enrolled in the program from other cities. The sooner he started the program, the closer he would get to his stay at one of the country's most coveted golf resorts and spas. Of course, in addition to the sun, he was excited about what the program could potentially do for his career. Nixon had seen firsthand how the benefit of strong networks could impact careers.

Nixon pulled in front of his mother's home, still tapping bass lines on his steering wheel. Gloria's begonias flanked the sides of the steps leading to her front door, vibrant balls of burgundy and rose. Twisted bushes stood proudly behind them, while a rosebush clung along the side of the railings. Nixon knew if he wasn't careful, it was easy to get pricked by one of those angry thorns if he reached for the rail without looking. The lush grass and neatly placed flowers gave life to the dull gray siding of the house beyond. It looked like someone full of time and love lived there.

Without actually smelling food, Nixon could smell his mother's cooking. Nostalgia had taken on a tangible essence. There was no way Gloria was cooking when her son was coming to take her to her favorite restaurant for lunch.

"Hi, Ms. Nelson!" Nixon waved at the elderly neighbor sitting on her porch, watering a small patch of bushes. For as long as Nixon had known Ms. Nelson, she'd been watering that same bunch of bushes and they still wouldn't grow.

"That you, Nixon?"

"Yes, Ms. Nelson." He remembered that she no longer could see or hear well.

"Oh. Good. Your mom has been waiting to see you."

"I know. You have a great day, okay?"

"Thank you, sweetheart."

Nixon hopped up the three brick steps leading to the front door. Before he could stick his key in the lock, the door opened. Gloria stood centered in the frame with her arms outstretched. Nixon stepped right between them and she wrapped those arms around him tightly.

"Hey, baby boy." Gloria pulled back, held him at arm's length and studied him the way mothers do. "You look like you're eating well." She cupped his face gently between her hands. "And you're still a handsome devil. Those girls in Long Island haven't been clamoring after you?" Gloria stepped aside so Nixon could enter fully.

"No, Ma. No clamoring." Nixon closed the door behind him.

"No 'person of interest' yet?"

"No, Ma." Nixon shook his head.

"Well, something has been keeping you from me. If you don't have time for your own mother—" she teased him with a slick smile, followed by a wink "—then at least take up with a nice girl. Work is great, but it will wear you out, leave you lonely and snatch time from under your feet. What good is it to die with a bank account full of money and no one to share your wealth or accomplishments with?"

"Ma!" Nixon moaned.

"Okay. I won't get on your nerves with the where-are-my-grandkids rant today. Fair?"

"Fair!" Nixon kissed her nose. He wanted to quell the inevitable as soon as possible.

This was how it always started, and soon enough it would end somewhere around the fact that she and his dad were responsible for ruining his perspective on commitment. It wasn't Gloria's fault that her husband had walked out, propelling them on a free fall into low-income living, until Gloria was innovative enough to climb out of the pit, with her job as an operator at the telephone company by day and the use of a sewing machine by night.

"I'm all ready to go. I just need to put a little lipstick on."

"Take your time, Ma." He said that because he knew she would. She always said she was going to put on a little lipstick and emerged at least a half hour later looking as though she was ready for a cover shoot. Who knew lipstick took so long to put on and was capable of making a woman look like she'd just been prepped for a cover shoot? Nixon chuckled to himself.

Despite the fact that they were going to have lunch soon, Nixon headed to the kitchen to see what was in the fridge. She'd already packed plastic containers filled with leftovers for him to take home. Nixon smiled, grabbed bottled water and closed the fridge. He'd have to remember not to go back to Long Island without his food. He'd finished up his last batch of home-cooked meals weeks before.

She'd taught him to cook and he did well, but still couldn't match her skills around a stove. He had a theory for what was missing. His mom loved cooking for him. He loved his mom, but who did he love cooking for? One day, he'd have someone in his life that he loved cooking for, and his meals would become as savory and perfect as his mother's.

The doorbell rang.

"Honey, can you get that, please?" His mother shouted from the powder room.

"Sure. You expecting anyone in particular?"

"No. It might be Ms. Nelson, if she needs something."

"Oh. Okay." Nixon trotted toward the door, careful not to leave Ms. Nelson waiting too long. "Hey." He'd already begun to greet her when he pulled the door open, but froze.

"Hey, son."

Nixon cleared his throat. "Hey." He didn't say "Dad." He wanted to, but didn't.

Nick Sr. had grown older since the year before. Lines creased his forehead, bags hung under his eyes, a shade darker than the rest of him, and silver-gray sprouts mixed in his silken, jet-black hair and beard. With his stature, he could have looked distinguished if he wasn't slumped and worn.

"Who is it, baby boy?"

Nixon realized neither he nor his father had moved a centimeter since he had opened the door.

"Hi, Gloria."

He'd saved Nixon from having to make the announcement. He was caught somewhere between saying it was "him," distancing himself from his father, and saying "your" ex-husband. He could have said "Dad," but sometimes that left a bitter taste on his tongue.

Nixon Sr.—or Nick, as most called him—looked down at the threshold, then back up at Nixon, as if silently asking for permission to enter. Nixon moved aside and Nick took two cautious steps, stopping just inside the door frame.

"Baby boy, did you hear me?" Gloria froze in place with an open tube of lipstick in her hand. "Nick? What brings you here?" There was surprise in Gloria's voice, but no malice. "How have you been?" She gave him a friendly hug and stepped back. Nixon caught the subtle way Gloria looked Nick over. "Have you eaten?"

"Oh." Nick waved his hand, politely declining her offer of a meal. "I'm fine. I was in the neighborhood and just stopped by. I know it's been a while." Nick spoke to Gloria, but glanced back at Nixon.

"Well, Nixon and I were just about to run out." Nixon perceived Gloria's statement as a cordial dismissal. She hadn't disclosed their plans or invited him to join them. "We'll be back by the evening. Will you still be in the area later?"

His father's large frame seemed drawn, Nixon thought. He stood there, head pinging back and forth between his parents, as they addressed one another in a casual manner that he himself couldn't seem to manage with his father. For some reason, he always felt like Nick was sizing him up.

Nixon busied himself doing nothing. When he looked up, Nick's eyes were on him again.

"Probably not," Nick said. "But it's a good thing I stopped by now." He turned to Nixon. "Haven't seen you in a while."

"Yeah."

"You're out on Long Island now, right?"

"Yeah."

"Like it?"

"It's nice." Nixon would tell his mother later, over lunch, about the house he was thinking of buying.

"Look." Nick swallowed. Nixon watched his throat shift like a lever. "I'm sorry about not showing up for dinner that day. Uh…something came up."

"Yeah." Nixon couldn't seem to find other words.

"Yeah," Nick replied in turn, his own voice more like a whisper. "Well, I'll get out of your way. I don't want to hold you two up."

"Okay." Gloria was heading back to the living room, her rhythmic footsteps a familiar sound. As a child, Nixon always knew when his mother was coming. "Let's chat later. I'll be around tonight."

"All right." Nick turned to leave. "Take care, son."

Nixon nodded his goodbye.

Gloria turned to Nixon. "You know he loves you, right?"

Nixon chuckled. He didn't know much about how his father felt about him. He didn't even know how *he* felt *himself.* Nixon wasn't exactly angry with his father for not being the dad he'd always wished for. But he wasn't numb to the complicated existence they shared, either. Interactions with Nick always left him feeling like a confused boy, desiring his father's attention, but not knowing what to do with it if he'd gotten it. As an adult, he'd tried pushing his feelings of rejection aside and reaching out to his father a couple times. It never worked out. He'd stopped trying.

Chapter 5

As usual, Jade was running short on time. She snatched her raincoat off the hanger dangling from her office door and shuffled to the car.

Jade chided herself for taking that last conference call on her office phone instead of her cell phone. She could have been halfway to the launch reception by now. She'd have to use the GPS system that alerted drivers of police presence so she'd know when to slow down on the expressway. If she sped just a little, she wouldn't be too noticeably late.

She'd been excited about the Executive Leadership Program when Ann told her about it, but when she received the official confirmation of her acceptance into the program by email, she was beside herself with anticipation. Jade was going to make her mark on the world as Jade Chandler, not just one of those Chandler girls. By no means would she ever balk at the benefits that came with carrying her family's name. She was proud to be a Chandler, but just needed to carve her own path.

"Dude! Move! The sign says stop, not stay!" Jade bore down on her horn, aware of how obnoxious she was being, but more aware of how the small window of time was slipping away from her. She wanted to be better at getting to places on time. It wasn't working tonight, but she was still going to try her best.

Jade made a quick pause at the stop sign and then attempted to get around the slow driver in front of her. When she saw that it was an elderly man, she felt bad. Embarrassed, she sank into her shoulders and lifted an apologetic hand as she zoomed past him. She made a left onto the expressway ramp and accelerated straight toward a solid wall of rush-hour traffic.

"Ugh!" She slapped the steering wheel, huffed and sat back. There was no chance she'd make it on time now.

Jade wanted to arrive early enough to scope out the other people in her cohort. Like most business events, it would start with twenty to thirty minutes of networking, she expected. She'd planned to look people up online via her phone in the parking lot, to see who they were and what companies they came from. But as she sat on the expressway, which resembled a parking lot, she knew there was no way to make that happen.

Who was there to blame but herself? Instead of stewing in irritation for the entire ride, Jade set the radio to a pop station and sang along with every song she knew. With a natural love for music, she had a thing for learning the words to her favorite songs. Music was more fun to listen to when you could sing along. Soon all her angst about being late melted away. She wasn't even annoyed about the fact that she'd spent at least ten miles driving at no more than five miles per hour. She was on target to arrive at least a half hour late.

Jade's tardy arrival at the country club was met by a plump young valet with a big smile and eyes full of promise. He gladly took her keys, promising to take good care of her "baby" as he squeezed behind the wheel and drove away.

Inside, she tried to enter quietly. Her heels clicked against the marble floor, giving her away. She tiptoed the rest of the way, avoiding contact between her spiked heels and the cold stone floor.

The woman at the registration table greeted her with a warm smile and whispered, "Welcome."

Jade returned the greeting just as warmly and looked for the badge bearing her name. She wasn't the only one late. She picked her badge up from the few still left scattered on the registration table.

Slowly, Jade pulled open the door to the banquet room where the reception was being held. A few heads turned in her direction. She hunched, as if hoping the people glancing over wouldn't see her. Jade held the door until it shut with a quiet click. A gentleman greeted her and led her to an open seat. Up front at the podium, a refined woman with jet-black roots and platinum tips sharply angled in an asymmetric haircut stood in a polished navy pencil dress. Cheerfully, she welcomed the new cohort. Jade was glad she'd dressed just as smartly.

In the next half hour, Jade learned more about the program, which was being sponsored by one of the local universities. Upon completion, participants would receive a coveted certification in executive leadership, she was glad to learn. Next they heard from recent graduates, who shared their experiences. By the time they were done with presenting all the information, Jade could hardly contain her enthusiasm. Her pulse thumped and a wide smile seemed to be permanently painted across her lips. The organizers ended the formal portion of the presentation by encouraging everyone in the room to continue networking before closing remarks were delivered.

Jade narrowed her vision on the last woman who'd spoken about her journey, and headed in her direction. On her way, she met a waiter carrying a tray with glasses of white wine, who silently offered her one. Jade reached out, but found her hand colliding with another person reaching for the same glass. The sudden contact caused a little wine to spill over the rim. Jade jumped back.

Shaking the liquid from her hand, she apologized. "I wasn't paying attention."

The waiter handed her a napkin. She wiped her fingers and finally looked up into a piercing set of brown eyes that actually made her breath catch. Seconds passed as she took him in, from his long masculine fingers to his well-fitting suit, sexy lips, neat mother-of-pearl teeth, smooth skin and finally those mesmerizing eyes that threatened to siphon her breath away, leaving her a vacant airless shell. *Damn!* She gathered herself, embarrassed. She shook her head. "Again, my apologies."

"No apologies necessary. Ladies first." The man picked up a glass and handed it to her. Jade's sight fixed on his strong, dark hand as it drew closer to her. She averted her gaze when he lifted his eyes to meet hers and smiled. Suddenly, the room felt warmer. He reached back to get a glass for himself. With a nod, he held it up and then sipped.

"Thanks! Please excuse me." Jade angled her shoulder to pass between him and someone else standing nearby. For the first time, she felt how crowded the room was.

The breath-stealing man smiled as she walked away. She felt his eyes on her. Jade knew he was watching. She straightened her posture as she continued toward her target. When she finally wove her way there, a few other curious people surrounded the woman. She smiled at Jade, welcoming her into the conversation. The person next to Jade moved slightly, making room for her in the circle. The woman answered several questions about what she liked best about the program.

Jade got a chance to speak with her one-on-one and they exchanged business cards. Making her way around the room afterward, Jade spoke with more people, meeting some of her fellow program participants, previous grads, sponsoring company reps, facilitators and a few program coordinators. Before the night ended she'd collected more business cards and had spoken to most of the people in the room. Almost everyone except *him*. She purposely avoided talking to him. Well aware of his presence, she kept tabs on him through discreet glances. Jade noticed how the polished facades of some of the women all but dissolved under the magic of his dimpled smile. He had to be nothing but trouble. Jade wasn't there for trouble.

Chapter 6

He felt her before he saw her. Nixon stepped into the room and spotted the woman from the night before in the corner, pouring coffee and cream, and remembered the jolt he'd felt the night before when their hands touched. As he watched her this morning, Nixon felt a current prickle the surface of his skin. He looked down at his hand and wondered if she had felt it, too. Nothing like this had ever happened to him before. Not even with his ex-fiancée.

Though Nixon had avoided her, he'd watched her work the room last night. Occasionally, he had glanced over, swearing that she'd been looking his way. He wondered if she was part of the cohort or one of the facilitators. Being a fellow participant would put her close to him, and he didn't like the simple way her presence tested him. He was a ladies' man. Nixon wasn't interested in putting that aside yet. Not while he was having so much fun.

Doling out cheerful morning greetings, Nixon looked for his name on the tented cardstock and binders at each table. Facilitators, two of them, were posted at the front, and participants were seated around a large square grouping of tables. Nixon set his briefcase beside the chair in his designated spot and headed to the table holding a heaping pile of bagels. He grabbed one loaded with sesame seeds. Hanging back, he waiting for his mystery woman to move away from the table where coffee, tea and juice were set out. She stood there for a few more moments, chatting with another woman.

Nixon noticed that this woman wasn't smartly dressed in business gray or navy, like most of the other women. Her clothes were less formal, more stylish, with a slightly rebellious edge—an eclectic combination of business and personality. The bun piled at the crown of her head, the soft pink shirt with the peekaboo view of her bare shoulders, her dress pants and chic hot-pink heels told Nixon that she conformed to her own standards.

Her scent hit him. It was just like he'd remembered—a floral aroma. Pleasant. Nixon's stomach rumbled. Was he hungry or was that reaction triggered by the memory of her scent? Quickly, he poured a cup of black coffee and returned to his spot with his bagel and a small serving of cream cheese. Tearing his focus away from her, he dived in on his bagel. She came and sat next to him. The tent card in front of her read Jade Chandler.

Jade Chandler. Nixon spoke the name in his head. Politely, she nodded and said a cool "Good morning," as if she had heard him.

"Good morning." He held his hand out. "Nixon Gaines."

She had a strong handshake and her touch made that sensation rise up on his skin again.

"Nice to meet you." She turned her attention to the coffee and croissant in front of her.

"Jade Chandler, huh?" Nixon lifted a brow and nodded. He had repeated her name just to taste it on his lips.

His mother cautioned him about women who had a certain effect on a man. Their lure was like the sticky silk of a spider's web. Nixon couldn't pull his attention away for too long. Jade challenged the ladies' man in him. Only moments ago, he'd learned her name, said it and wanted to say it again.

"Good morning and welcome!" The voice boomed from a mature stout woman standing in front of the room. Her cheerful greeting caught everyone's attention. She clapped her hands together. "We're so excited to have you as our inaugural cohort for the Long Island region. The next several weeks—or months, I should say—will be both intense and thrilling. We have so much in store for you and look forward to what we will also learn from you. We'll start by going around the room and introducing ourselves." She gave instructions on what everyone should include in their introduction: names, titles, companies and one thing that each person expected to get out of the program.

Nixon was grateful that the facilitator suggested the introductions start from the opposite side of the room. That would give him time to figure out the one thing he wanted to get from the program. He was so caught up in his thoughts he only half listened to what the others had to say. His turn came around faster than he'd expected.

He stood. Nodded. "Nixon Gaines." He delivered the rest of the information he'd been asked for, tugged on his suit jacket and sat. "I'm looking forward to growing professionally, building relationships and expanding my network."

"Thank you, Nixon," the facilitator said.

Jade rose to her feet beside him. He took in every inch of her as she stretched to her full height. His eyes swept up, down and back up her side until they landed on her smooth cheek. Jade addressed the room. Nixon wasn't sure why the name of her foundation sounded so familiar.

Nixon watched her as she returned to her seat, and turned away right before he could be accused of staring too long. What was it about her?

Next, the group dived into a leadership activity that continued for the next few hours, nonstop, until lunch. Nixon was thankful because he knew that at any moment, his stomach would voice its discontentment for having to wait so long to eat. The last thing he needed was for Jade to be subjected to that angry rumbling.

Lunch was served in the adjacent room. He still hadn't said anything more to Jade, but kept her in his view. Most of the participants moved about in a more familiar manner now that the first half of the day had passed. They mixed and mingled, getting to know a little more about one another, yet he and Jade operated like opposite ends of a magnet. Wherever he was in the room, Jade was sure to be on the other side.

"Nixon? Right?"

He turned to find a voluptuous woman with a head full of honey-colored curls. She held her hand out. They shook and she held his hand a moment longer than what could be considered professional.

"Yes. And you are?" he asked.

"Julia. Julia Riggs."

"Yes!" Nixon only half remembered. Jade had hijacked his attention and he wasn't sure he liked that. Normally, he would have taken notice of a woman like Julia. He laid a heap of mixed green salad on his plate.

"So you're in business development, right?" Julia asked.

"Yes. You remembered." He applauded her with his tone.

"Remembering is one of the many things I'm really good at."

Nixon wondered if it was his imagination or if Julia had just lifted her ample bust slightly higher. He knew when a woman was flirting with him. Usually he'd indulge, if only just for the fun of it. He loved a woman who wasn't afraid to go after something she wanted. But today, he was being cautious. He wouldn't jump on what she was dangling. He looked around to see where Jade was.

Nixon chuckled. "That's great. Nice meeting you." He flashed his most charming smile, finished adding items to his lunch plate and headed to a table on the opposite side of the room. Natural light poured through the windows by his table. From his vantage point, he could see the entire space. Nixon liked it there. He could glance at Jade and keep abreast of anything else going on around him.

"Can I join you?" A coy smile was fixed on Julia's face.

Nixon held his hand out, gesturing for her to sit. "Sure." He looked for Jade again. She looked right back at him. For a second, their gazes locked. She looked away first. Julia had missed it. And he missed whatever she was saying.

"Daydreaming or just have a lot on your mind?" Julia asked.

"Huh? Oh. A lot on my mind, I guess."

She snickered. "So tell me more about you, Mr. Gaines."

Nixon tried to keep the conversation light. His responses were basic and cordial. They discussed former

jobs, outside affiliations and the schools they'd most re-
cently graduated from. She leaned closer over the table-
top as if she wanted to prevent missing any of his words.
But her intentions were palpable. Nixon sat back, adding
a little distance between them. When it was Julia's turn
to share, she purred as she spoke. Her mannerisms were
flirty and fluid, as if she had liquid in her bones, and
she spoke in innuendos. Several statements held double
meanings. She was opening the door. All Nixon had to
do was step in. But he held back, surprised at his own
response. When he finished eating, he politely excused
himself.

The facilitators called everyone back into the main
room for the second half of the day, which started with
a team-building exercise. They were separated into two
groups. He, Jade and Julia ended up in the same one.
One of the facilitators gave them a square tarp. Each
team had to figure out how to stand on the tarp and turn
it over without stepping off it. The first team to figure
it out would get a prize. It was a brainteaser that forced
the six people on each team to put their heads together
and their bodies even closer.

As they maneuvered the tarp under their feet, they had
less to stand on. Their grouping tightened until they stood
shoulder to shoulder. Julia shimmied against his arm.
Something similar to an electric current shivered down
his other arm. Without looking to that side, he knew that
Jade's body had connected with his. Even through their
clothes, she managed to generate currents. It wasn't his
imagination. What was it with this woman?

Their team successfully completed the task first. Everyone cheered. Nixon held his palms high, slapping hands,
waiting for Jade's to connect with his. Julia was the first to
give him a high five. When Jade finally did, she avoided

his eyes and quickly returned to her seat. He knew that energy. He understood all at once. All day Jade had evaded him in the same fashion that he'd attempted to avoid her. Like opponents, they held to opposite sides of the room, spoke cordially to everyone around but each other and failed miserably at avoiding eye contact. Nixon could count how many times he'd glanced at her and found her already discreetly looking his way, or vice versa. Like him, she was trying not to get sucked in by the mysterious magnetism that threatened to collapse their resolve if they got too close. Nixon couldn't help but smile at the realization. He already knew that a connection with this woman would be inevitable.

The facilitators congratulated the winning group and asked everyone to return to their seats. They announced how the groups would work together on a major project. Of course, Jade ended up on his team. Nixon was going to see more of Jade than he'd expected.

Chapter 7

Once their day session ended, Jade offered quick salutations and made a swift exit. She started the car and pulled out before anyone else from her cohort could make it outside.

Nixon Gaines. He was watching her all day, just like he'd watched her the night before. Jade chuckled. She wouldn't have known that he was watching her if she wasn't watching him, too. Her chuckle blossomed into a full laugh. Who was she fooling? No matter how hard she tried, she couldn't keep herself from looking at his handsome face, tall taut frame and suave mannerisms. Surely he was a sculptured work of art under his well-made suit. He'd caught her watching a few times.

A horn blew behind her, breaking into her thoughts of Nixon. She carefully pressed the gas, drove on autopilot and pictured Nixon from the night before. Jade had seen him the moment she entered the room, his erect posture commanding the space around him as if he were its ruler. Even from the back she could tell he was gorgeous. His broad shoulders and slim waist had carried his stylish ensemble like a model.

Jade had also noticed how all eyes were on Nixon. Even today, several women, including the female facilitators, couldn't seem to resist looking at him every chance they got. But the woman with the headful of curls made her intentions perfectly clear. Jade figured she was making her move before anyone else could lay claim to Nixon.

Despite Nixon being an indulgent distraction, Jade had come for business. Carving her own professional legacy was her priority. She'd seen good-looking men before. Let the other women in the program have at him. Just like today, she'd continue to avoid him.

Jade turned onto the Northern State Parkway, determined to rid herself of thoughts about Nixon. Even though it was close to the end of the workday, she headed toward the office to get a few things done before going home. She was sure that a few folks from her staff would still be around.

Jade hit the home button on her cell and instructed the phone to call her cousin Kendall. Their conversation would keep her company during her ride.

"Hey." Kendall's greeting seemed dry.

"What's wrong?"

Kendall's breathy huff came across the line. "This has not been the best of days."

"Feel like talking?" Jade hated to hear Kendall sound so down.

"Got a few hours?" Kendall said, using their quip for big issues.

"Always for you."

Kendall shared the drama she was experiencing in her

relationship. Jade listened intently, waiting patiently for her cue on how to respond. If Kendall sounded as if she were near tears, Jade would keep her opinions to herself and let her vent. Then Jade thought about the bad decisions she'd made with Mitch and decided she wasn't in a place to deliver sound relationship advice anyway.

"How do you feel now?" Jade asked, after Kendall went silent.

"It's hard to say. In this industry, anything we do can be misinterpreted. If I go to lunch with a producer to talk about a potential project, someone is likely to take a picture on their cell phone and post to social media. The next thing you know, rumors start and bloggers are posting 'exclusives' about 'who's dating who.' It's crazy. So if there's really something going on with him and another woman, I need to approach it the right way."

"Wow. That sucks!"

"I know, but that's entertainment. Let's talk about something more exciting. How's your life?"

"Exciting? Ha! You're the big-time pop artist living in Los Angeles, California." Jade announced the city as if she were about to start a performance and wanted to wrangle the crowd. "There's no way my life can be more exciting than yours. I did have my first class today."

"Yeah? How did it go?"

"Great!"

"Any cuties in the program?"

Nixon's face popped into her mind. Kendall had to ask. "Well, since you asked…" Jade chuckled and told her about Nixon.

"Mmm. He sounds yummy."

"Oh, he's very yummy, but this girl's hunger is for much more than a gorgeous guy. I've got my eye on the prize—making a name for myself professionally. Besides, the competition is thick. Every woman in the program, facilitators included, couldn't seem to keep their eyes off him. It's almost embarrassing. One girl was all over him when we broke for lunch today. Trust that I will keep my distance."

"Oh. He's one of those."

"Yeah. Big-time playboy, it seems."

"Steer clear!" Kendall warned. "You see what I'm dealing with."

"Yeah. Oh." Another thought came. Jade paused a moment. "I saw Mitch again." When she finally spoke again, her voice was lower.

After several moments, Kendall asked, "And?"

"It was okay. We spoke. He hugged me. I wanted to ask about his *fiancée* but didn't."

"That's probably best." They sighed at the same time and then laughed at how in sync they were. "It doesn't look like we have much luck with men."

"I know. Do you think we'll ever have what our parents have?"

"I really don't know. You probably have a better chance than me. Tinseltown is rough on love lives."

Jade's call to her cousin was supposed to distract her in a good way, not make her mood more somber. She ended her call with Kendall at the same time that she pulled into the parking lot. At the foundation, which was housed in a different part of the Chandler Foods campus from her family, Jade ran a staff of less than ten. The corporate side employed several hundred people. Even though her father, sister and brother worked on the same campus, she hardly ever saw them.

Jade mustered up a cheerful greeting for the receptionist and made her way down the corridor to the Chandler Foundation's office. The moment she stepped in, she noticed something was different. The closer she got to her own office, the more she could feel it. Jade worked hard to create a culture where her team seemed more like a family. And just like with family, she could sense when something wasn't quite right.

The quiet was intense, replacing the usual hum of busy bodies hard at work and the rumble of employee banter. Even the background music system played into the solemn atmosphere, releasing a sad-sounding tune throughout the space. She found most of her staff hovered inside the office of her program director.

"What's going on?" Several pairs of eyes stared back at her and then landed on the program director.

"Hey, boss lady," another employee said, her tone confirming that things were off.

Other employees had similar greetings. Their faces matched their tones.

"We will get out of here so you two can talk," said the staff member who had taken a liking to calling her "boss lady," and she shuffled the others out the door. They closed it behind them.

Jade looked back at her program director, Sandy, seated behind her desk. Sandy's face was drawn. Sadness filled the worried lines around her mouth. Red squiggly lines crossed in the whites of her eyes.

Jade sat, bracing herself for the bad news that was obviously coming. Her heart swelled for whatever it was that was causing Sandy distress.

Sandy looked at Jade, took a breath and opened her mouth. Instead of words coming out, her mouth trembled and tears began to flow. Jade rounded the desk and took her into her arms. Together they rocked until the quaking caused by Sandy's crying subsided. Jade took Sandy's hands in hers.

"Talk to me, Sandy."

"It's my mother. She…" Sandy sniffed back another sob. "She's ill and I have to go."

"Oh no!" Jade moaned, squeezing her hands tighter. "I'm so sorry. Go. Do whatever you have to do. We'll cover everything while you're gone. Take as much time as you need."

Sandy's shoulders drooped. She shook her head. "No. I mean I have to leave."

"Yes." Confused, Jade frowned. "Your mother lives in Virginia, right? You need to go to her. I understand that. It's no problem."

"Jade." Sandy swallowed. Jade saw the muscles in her neck shift. "I'm not coming back."

"Wh-what? Sandy!"

"I'm so sorry, Jade." Tears began to flow again.

Sandy's words didn't compute. She didn't know what to say. Sandy had been with her since she became executive director. They were as close as friends could be when one was the boss.

Jade sat slowly. "What happened?"

"My mother's illness is terminal and there's nothing more the doctors can do. They discovered it too late. She only has a few months and I need to be with her. I'm an only child, so everything is on me." Sandy cried into her hands.

Jade nodded. Her own tears began to flow. She could only imagine what Sandy was going through and couldn't imagine having to stomach that same fate alone. At least she had her siblings.

"I'm so sorry, Sandy." The two of them stood, hugged and cried for some time together.

"Tell me what you need. How can I help? What can I do?"

Sandy chuckled through the tears. "Right now, I don't even know."

Jade laughed with her for a short moment. "When you figure it out, I'll be right here."

They embraced again and then heard a knock at the door. Another employee stuck her head in.

"Come on in here." Jade waved to her. The rest of their team poured in right behind her, gathering around them in one large group hug, with Jade and Sandy in the center.

It broke Jade's heart to see Sandy so sad. She hated the fact that her program director, colleague—friend—had to go. She wondered what part of her executive leadership training would help with situations like this. Jade didn't want to think about how losing Sandy would impact work, but couldn't help wondering how things would get done without her—especially their big fund-raiser coming up for the holidays. Every single staff member played a role in coordinating the event. She could find a new program director, but she'd never find another Sandy.

Chapter 8

Nixon looked up just as Alex stepped into his office.

"Morning, Mr. Brentworth."

He dismissed Nixon's formal greeting with a wave. "Alex," he said, taking a seat across from his desk.

"Morning, Alex." Nixon adjusted with a nod. "How are you?"

"Well. Very well, and yourself?"

"Well."

Alex sat back in his usual authoritative way. The confidence he exuded commanded respect. Nixon cleared his throat and sat straighter.

"How's the program going?"

Now Nixon relaxed. There was a lot that he liked about this program. It was intense. No amount of coaching had offered Nixon so much insight on being an effective leader. They covered material that even his MBA program hadn't touched upon. The connections he'd begun to make were priceless. And then he thought of Jade. "Absolutely great!"

"I'm glad to hear it." Alex leaned forward. "Listen. Do you have a woman in your program named Jade Chandler?"

Nixon hid his surprise. How did they know about Jade? "Actually, yes. Why do you ask?"

"Do you know her well?"

"I know that she's very much invested in the program. She doesn't speak much." Nixon thought about whether or not he should mention that he'd see her later that day. Their group was getting together to work on their team project. "What makes you ask?"

"You know Chandler Foods, right?"

Of course Nixon knew. It was his business to know the other companies in his industry. It hit him. "She's one of *those* Chandlers." His eyes widened. Nixon hadn't made that connection, but recalled her saying that she worked for the Chandler Foundation. That was why it sounded so familiar. Had she said Chandler Foods, he would have made the connection immediately.

"Yes. I heard that she was in the program."

Nixon waited a beat for Alex to say more, but he didn't. "I assume you know the Chandlers?"

"I've become more familiar with them as of late." Alex stood. "Glad you're enjoying the program. Keep me posted." He tugged on the front of his suit jacket, swiped an invisible piece of lint off his shoulder and headed toward the door. "Good day, Nixon. Keep up the great work."

"Good day, Alex," Nixon said to his retreating back. He watched Alex walk out. There was obviously more to Alex's line of questioning than he'd let on. Rather than dwell on that, Nixon returned his attention to the strategic partnership proposal he'd been working on before Alex's visit. But thoughts of the inquisition didn't wane. Through the remainder of the afternoon, Nixon wondered what was behind Alex's line of questioning. However, with an impending deadline facing him and all the prep he needed to complete for his team's meeting later that evening, he had no choice but to put aside the queries rising in his consciousness.

Nixon put his head into his proposal as much as he could before heading home to get ready for the meeting with his project team. He considered working late and going straight from his office, but thought better of that idea. He needed to freshen up—get the workday off him, since he was going to see Jade. Alex's interest in Jade made her more intriguing. Nixon decided to look her up online before he left the office. Her social media confirmed what he'd already summed up about her.

With all the zany family pictures he perused, it was obvious that Jade was family oriented. Nothing about her social life was lacking, and she knew how to vacation. She was stylish. And as he had expected, it seemed she was involved in several community organizations. She was beautiful and she had great personality, it seemed. He knew social media offered only the highlight reel of her life, and he wanted to see what the camera didn't show.

"Whoa! Easy, cowboy." He admonished himself aloud, holding his palms in the air like he was pressing against a wall. Had he just imagined them together?

Nixon shut his computer down and headed home for a fresh restart for the second part of his day.

Sometime later, Nixon pulled up to the gate and gave his name to the bright-eyed young man with the neat goatee. Chandler Foods was more like a campus than just an office complex. There were two buildings a few stories tall that were connected by a skywalk and a central courtyard. The courtyard boasted a large fountain, benches and greenery that was still lush from the summer. Fall temperatures hadn't become bitter enough to destroy the vibrant beauty of the colorful flowers. Nixon assumed one structure was the warehouse where all those tasty baked goods were made and stored before being distributed to supermarkets across the globe, and that the other housed the offices.

Following the guard's directions, Nixon steered around the building on the left to where the Chandler Foundation offices resided. Pulling into a parking spot, Nixon shut off the engine and sat back a moment. He was early, but had planned it that way. He texted Jade as he walked toward the door, just as she had asked them to do when they arrived. After business hours, visitors without passkeys couldn't enter the building.

Several moments went by before Jade arrived, wearing blue jeans, a white button-down shirt, a bright blue blazer and pumps of the same hue, looking more chic than professional.

"Hey. You made it." Jade smiled and held out her hand for a shake. Nixon glanced at it for a quick moment and then clasped it. Again, he felt a light wave of electricity when their palms touched. "You found the place without issue?" Jade pulled her hand away quickly and stepped aside to let him into the building.

Nixon smiled. The only way she didn't feel that was if she was postmortem. "Yes, I did. I have a few clients in the area."

Jade headed down the hall, her heels clicking quickly against the tiled floor. Nixon followed, his long legs allowing him to keep up. He was thankful that she'd continued to avoid eye contact with him. Had she been more comfortable, she would have caught him trying not to notice how perfectly those jeans fitted the curve of her hips or how the heels made her legs look tight and lean. He admired her shape.

The walk down the corridor toward her area was quiet. She pushed through glass doors with steel letters bearing the foundation's name and led Nixon into the conference room, which was an average-sized space with more glass doors, near-white walls and a fairly large white table with high-backed gray chairs surrounding it.

Nixon looked around. "I'm the first to arrive." It was more of a confirmation than a statement.

"Yep. Would you like something to drink?" Jade busied herself removing the plastic wrap that covered a platter of fruit and one with cheese and crackers. She still hadn't looked directly at him.

"Water will be fine." Nixon grabbed one of the half-pint-sized water bottles lined up by the platters.

"I just figured I'd provide a little something. We also have coffee and tea in the kitchen."

"Coffee sounds good."

"Right this way." She signaled for him to follow her.

Nixon did so, holding in a chuckle from the formal cool shoulder she was giving him. He'd kept feeling that same sensation every time their skin touched. Nixon knew she had to have felt it, too. She'd pulled her hand back from that handshake a moment ago as if she'd touched fire. He also knew she had to notice the static electricity that seemed to buzz between them whenever they stood too close. He wanted to touch her again just to feel the current.

Still avoiding eye contact, Jade popped a cup in the coffeemaker and watched as the brown liquid streamed into it with a gurgle and a hiss. She passed the steaming cup to Nixon, carefully trying to avoid skin-to-skin contact.

"Careful. It's hot. The cream and sugar are over there."
She jutted her chin in the direction of the refrigerator.

"Thanks," Nixon said, taking the cup from her hand.
He made sure he grazed her fingers in the transfer. A
light jolt scampered across his hand and he liked it. A lot.

Jade cleared her throat and hurried to the other side of
the contemporary kitchen, which had light-colored wood
cabinets and bistro seating throughout. Nixon followed
her. Until that moment she'd been professional—more
like cool and distant. Jade grabbed a handful of individual creamer cups and a few packs of sugar, placed
them on a small paper plate and turned, bumping right
into Nixon's chest. She nearly bounced off. The sudden
contact made her look directly at him for the first time.
Jade flinched and froze for a tiny portion of a second,
but it was long enough for Nixon to confirm that she felt
the same thing he did.

"I'm sorry. I didn't realize you were so close."

"My apologies. I was coming for the cream." Nixon
decided immediately that his choice of words wasn't the
best, but he let them hang there. Pulling back could make
it seem as if he'd meant to offer an innuendo, and that
wasn't his style. When he flirted, it was evident. Nixon
wasn't one to hide behind words.

Jade made herself a cup of coffee, poured in two packs
of cream and headed back toward the conference room.
The start time for the meeting had come and no one else
had arrived. Nixon couldn't imagine that all four of them
were late.

Jade looked at her watch. "I'm sure they'll be here
any minute." She busied herself again, rearranging the
same trays that she'd set in place before they went into
the kitchen. Nervous energy sizzled around her.

Nixon placed his coffee cup on the table and walked

to where she stood by the food. He filled a small plate with cheese and crackers. Jade finished fiddling with the trays and turned. Nixon was right there.

"We never had the chance to really talk. After these few weeks, I feel like I know everyone in the program except you."

"Yeah. I keep to myself. I really want to get the most out of this program."

Nixon tilted his head and looked at her as if he were peering over a pair of reading glasses. For a quick moment, Jade looked confused.

"Yeah, I knew you were the quiet type." Sarcasm dripped off each word.

Jade's mouth opened, then closed. "Wha…" Her laugh bubbled through her full lips, almost involuntarily, it seemed.

Nixon joined her. He'd called her on her avoidance and she knew her cover had been blown. The fact that there was no fight in her made him laugh harder.

Nixon put his plate down, looked her directly in the eye for the first time and asked, "Why have you been avoiding me? I don't bite."

Jade closed her eyes, smiled and sighed. "I don't avoid you. I just…keep my distance."

"Why?" Nixon knew why. It was for the same reason that he'd become so intrigued by her. Something magnetic clung to them when they were around each other, drawing them close, forcing them to pile space between them so they wouldn't be consumed by its pull. This was all unfamiliar to Nixon. He hadn't even felt this in his ex-fiancée's presence. It was exhilarating. Scary. It challenged the player in him and made his usual smooth charm seem spastic.

Jade twisted her lips from one side to the other. She

exhaled audibly and then opened her mouth to answer, but her cell phone rang. She looked at the display. It was Julia. Jade simply turned the phone toward him so he could see the name. "This is why?"

Answering the call, Jade turned, exited the conference room and headed toward the entrance. Nixon heard her say, "Okay. I'll be at the door by the time you get there."

When Jade left the room, Nixon huffed. "Damn," he said under his breath.

Chapter 9

Jade wasn't sure whether or not she was relieved when Julia called to say she was outside. Trying to avoid noticing Nixon was hard work. Who could ignore his majestic stature, slightly bowed legs, slim waist, broad taut chest, the regal jut of his strong chin, plump kissable lips, sexy dimpled smile, piercing brown eyes and unreasonably handsome face? She almost shuddered at the delicious mental list of his favorable attributes. His gorgeous body was always wrapped in stylish clothes that couldn't have been happier than to lie against skin that looked as if it had been dipped in creamy caramel. Nixon was great to look at—a work of art that belonged on display at the Smithsonian.

Jade reached the end of the corridor, rested her arm on the door handle and looked out at the rain dropping like slender shards of crystal. As she waited for Julia's car to come into view, she watched the rain blossom from a slim misty drizzle to a steady stream of heavy tear-shaped drops.

Jade's thoughts went back to Nixon. No matter how hard she tried not to look at him, she couldn't seem to keep her neck from craning in his direction. He was visually delectable. She kept needing just a little glance here and a little glance there. Had Nixon been a decadent dessert, she'd be in serious need of a dentist.

What truly made her keep her distance were all the other women she noticed glancing, too. A few, like Julia, were simply bold, slithering up against him as if something they needed was available only in the air around him. Others grinned in his face like they couldn't control their girl-crush impulses. All that overexertion of femininity and pheromones made her want to stay away.

Jade hadn't missed how he'd been looking at her. Every time she attempted to steal a glance, he had caught her. The popular cute guy had never been her thing. Instead, Jade dashed in the opposite direction when a man tossed about his irresistible flair or player ways, preferring more solid interactions. She was direct and specific. The tired dance these men played when they were trying to charm women irritated her. Either you wanted to date or not, have sex or not, be committed or not.

Her no-nonsense, all-black, no-gray candor with men *had* earned her a few regrets. Mitch had by far been her biggest regret. Jade walked away thinking they weren't on the same page. Once he was gone, she wanted to be on whatever page she'd left him on, but it was too late.

A time or two, she'd been guilty of stepping away from a relationship prematurely after getting the impression that her date was losing interest. Some called after her, wondering why she'd disappeared from their lives so suddenly. She could never be accused of being the clingy type.

Jade hadn't seen Julia pull up, but she did see her waving wildly as she dashed through the rain. Julia's coat covered her head.

Jade swept her passkey by the security pad. Rapid flashing red lights turned to green. After the click, Jade opened the door. "Hi, Julia. Glad you made it."

"Whew!" Julia hurried inside. "I didn't know they called for rain." She shook water from her hands and let her coat slide back into place. Julia swung her head from side to side, righting her curls and patting them. "Hi." She released another breath. "Can I use the bathroom?"

"Sure." Jade started down the hall. "Right this way. Wanna put your coat and bag down first?"

"Yeah." Soggy and hunched, Julia traipsed into the conference room.

"Sit wherever you want."

"Okay," Julia said.

Jade waited for her to put her belongings on a chair so she could show her to the restroom.

"Hey, Julia," Nixon said.

Julia's head snapped up. She went from hunched to standing erect. Her breasts rose higher, revealing cleavage. The harried expression she came in with morphed into a sultry smile. "Hey, Nixon," she sang, with a delicate lift of her chin. "You made it here before me, I see. There was an accident right in front of me. My goodness. I saw the whole thing happen. That's what held me up. I'm sure the others are right behind me." Julia patted her curls again, then slid her hands down the sides of her torso and hips.

"Didn't you have to go to the bathroom?" Jade asked, thinking Julia may have forgotten that and the fact that Jade was still in the room.

"Oh. Yes." She snickered. "Be right ba-a-ack." Instead of walking, she wiggled out of the room.

Jade rolled her eyes and chuckled under her breath. Julia was obviously smitten by Nixon. She showed Julia where the restroom was and returned to the conference room.

Nixon simply smirked. Jade's phone rang again. She looked at the display and headed for the door. The three remaining team members had arrived at the same time. Jade was relieved that she wouldn't have to make another trip down the corridor to open the door after this.

Shaking rain from their outerwear, they exchanged greetings and followed Jade back to the conference room. Julia had moved her belongings and was now seated right next to Nixon. She was marking her territory. A fleeting feeling of jealousy shot through Jade. Then she shook her head, ridding herself of that ridiculous reaction.

Her mind went back to the private moments she and Nixon had shared before the others came, and wished they'd had a little more time together. Both their guards were temporarily down. Once he called her on her behavior, Jade had felt comfortable being alone with him. That space was all theirs.

She repelled the thought as soon as it came. The last thing she needed in this program was a distraction—especially one as tall, gorgeous and sexy as Nixon.

Jade cleared her throat and returned to being the cool professional. "The bathroom and kitchen are down the hall. There's coffee, tea, and I have some nibbles for us right here. Get dry and settled and we can start when you're ready." With the others in the room, she returned to avoiding eye contact with Nixon.

"Thanks, Jade," her teammates said at once.

"It was nice of you to offer your space," Sammy said. "I'm just going to grab a cup of coffee and I'll be right back, ready to jump in. That cool?"

"Cool with me," Jade said. In recent weeks, she had gotten used to the rhetorical way Sammy added "that cool?" to the end of his sentences. He wasn't seeking permission.

For the next two hours, the group brainstormed ideas for their group project, to the thunderous symphony of rain slamming against the glass walls like drums. Julia seemed to love every one of Nixon's ideas. She purred, cooed and giggled after every phrase that fell from his lips. Playfully, she'd swat his arm or gently place her hand over his.

Jade could tell that the group was growing tired of Julia's overt flirtation. Quick, uncomfortable glances ping-ponged between them at first, but soon after, eyes blatantly rolled and tongues clucked. Their expressions of frustration went from discreet, knowing nods over her behavior to huffs and comments like "Julia, focus," or "Geesh," which Sammy often repeated. Nixon handled the extra attention with a delicate balance—not feeding into her antics, but not ignoring her altogether, either. Unfazed, he seemed like the only one not distracted by Julia.

Jade was glad when the two hours were up, and dreaded having to deal with this over the next several weeks as the group worked on the project together.

Sammy yawned. "Whew! Excuse me." He covered his mouth, stood and gathered his belongings. "I think we made good progress." He opened his eyes wide. "Could have made more." His nod toward Julia was subtle. Everyone but Julia noticed. She was busy talking to Nixon. "But I'd say we did pretty good despite…" He let his thought end there—no need to say any more.

"I agree," Jade said. Everyone else nodded.

"So next week?" Nixon asked.

They looked at each other for confirmation, agreeing with nods, shrugs and verbal affirmations.

"I can host again," Jade offered.

"That would be great! But we shouldn't wear out our welcome here. Let's rotate," Nixon suggested.

"We can meet at my office next," Sammy said. "I'm actually not too far from here." Everyone agreed.

They exchanged good-nights and started off on their separate ways.

"Let me help you clean up," Nixon said, picking up empty cups and scrunched napkins from the conference table.

"Yeah. I'll help, too." Julia grabbed some stuff and tossed it in the garbage.

"Thanks, but I can take care of it."

"Okay." Julia placed the cup in her hand back on the table and slid her sleeve inside her coat. "I guess I'll see you next week, Jade." She picked up her purse and turned to Nixon. "Are you walking out?"

"Not yet."

"Oh." Julia looked disappointed. "I'll wait for you."

Jade rolled her eyes as she carried the fruit tray to the garbage.

"No need. I'm going to help Jade clean up and see her to her car."

"I'm sure Jade will be fine. She works here. She goes to her car every day without a problem."

Jade stopped moving. She took the inside of her lip between her teeth and gnawed gently. She did that to keep from commenting about Julia speaking about her as if she weren't present.

"How about this? I'll walk you to your car now, come back and get Jade to make sure she gets to her car, and then I'll know that both you ladies are safe."

Julia lifted her shoulders, giggled and placed her hand on his chest. "You're such a gentleman. 'Bye, Jade. Thanks for hosting."

"'Bye, Julia!" Jade's cheerful salutation was Oscar-worthy. She shook her head and noticed Nixon's small smile when he looked her way.

While Nixon went off to carry out his gentlemanly duties, Jade cleared the rest of the space. She gathered her coat and headed down the corridor. She opened the door to walk out, and Nixon walked in.

"You're all ready?"

"Yep."

Nixon tilted his head toward the meeting room. "I left my notes in there."

Jade held them up between her index finger and thumb. "You mean these?"

"Thanks!"

"Now, could you be a gentleman and walk me to my car, Mr. Gaines?" Jade batted her eyes, mimicking Julia's tone.

"Ha!" Nixon wagged his finger at Jade. "On one condition."

Jade scrunched her brow.

"After that meeting, I could use a drink. Join me?" Jade was just about to protest when Nixon added, "It could be coffee if that makes you more comfortable. But I prefer wine."

Jade thought for another moment. "Sure." What could it hurt? "Let's get some wine."

Nixon's perfect lips spread into a sexy grin. Jade wasn't sure he was capable of smiling without it looking sexy.

"Great! I know a great place. You can follow me."

The two of them trotted through the rain and hurried into their cars. Jade wanted to decline Nixon's offer, but her desire to go was stronger. She couldn't keep avoiding him. Soon that would begin to look as obvious as Julia's flirting. Plus, she liked being around him. They could become friends. Getting to know him better would make him less of a distraction—put those giddy butterfly tremors in her belly to rest.

Perhaps she'd even find out something about him that knocked him down a peg, and he wouldn't seem like such a handsome demigod. Familiarity made people and things lose luster. He'd become normal to her, and maybe, just maybe, her skin would no longer tingle when he came close.

Chapter 10

The British voice of Nixon's GPS announced that he'd reached his destination. Nixon personally claimed the robotic guide as his Brit.

He pulled up next to a parking spot close to the entrance of the wine bar he favored on Northern Boulevard, turned on his interior light and gestured toward the open space before pulling off. Jade got the message and pulled into the spot.

Once they were inside, it took a few minutes for them to be seated. They squeezed past the bar teeming with noisy patrons and waded through the loud jazz music streaming from the speakers. Nixon and Jade were seated along the wall near the center of the wine bar. From that vantage point, he could see the entire place.

Nixon finally had her alone. He could find out who Jade really was. There was no Julia competing for his attention. The more other women peddled their presence, the further Jade distanced herself. She'd hardly spoken to Nixon during their weekly sessions.

At first Nixon just looked at Jade sitting across the table from him. Drank her in while she scanned the bar from one side to the other. Even in the dim light her beauty was illuminated. Nixon wanted to reach over and slide aside the strand of hair loosened from her bun. He kept his hand on the table—studied her some more. Large doe eyes gave Jade an air of innocence. Long lashes made her appear to bat her eyes every time she blinked. Luscious pink lips eased into a shy smile when she caught him staring.

"This is a nice place," she said, turning toward the other side. "It reminds me a little of my brother's place."

"It's one of my favorites. Your brother has a place like this?"

Jade nodded.

"I'll have to try it out one of these days."

"Tapas," she said matter-of-factly, picking up the menu. "Any good?"

"Delicious. May I?" Nixon opened the menu.

"You think you know me well enough to order for me?"

"I can try. Maybe I'll impress you."

"I'm not easily impressed."

"That doesn't have to stop me from trying."

Jade smirked. 'Touché." She sliced the air with her finger like a sword.

The waiter checked in. Jade ordered cabernet and Nixon asked for merlot and a few options off the tapas menu.

"What should I know about you, Jade Chandler?"

"What do you want to know, Nixon Gaines?"

"Anything you're willing to tell. Your secrets are safe with me."

Jade pursed her lips and tilted her head sideways. "Really, Nixon." He laughed. "Then you'll have to wait until I have a glass or two of wine."

"Ha! Waiter!" Nixon held his finger up.

This time Jade laughed, but her playful statement held an element of truth. After a glass of wine and some tasty tapas, Jade seemed more relaxed to Nixon. If he wanted to know more about her, he figured it made sense to reveal a few things about himself, as well.

"I love movies and muscle cars. I wanted to be an actor until I grew up and realized I sucked at acting. I couldn't hold a tune even if it were strapped to my body with a harness, and I love my mama. Your turn." Nixon sipped his wine.

"Oh. Well… I like movies, too, more than regular television. I don't pay much attention to cars. I'm great at chess. Love playing cards. Thought about modeling but knew it would never fly with my mom—whom I also love. I come from a musically gifted family. My older sister sings like a beautiful bird. My other sister could really give Tiger a run for his titles on the golf course and my brother plays multiple instruments." She sipped, punctuating the end of her list of characteristics. "Oh, and I love old-school R & B and rap music."

"Really? Ha! Me, too. Name some favorites."

"Anything from the eighties and nineties."

"'Poison' by—"

"BBD!" Jade shouted. Laughter bubbled from both of them.

"'This is how we do it.'" Nixon sang the famed line from a popular nineties party starter. His key was nowhere near correct.

Jade covered her ears. "Oh. You really can't sing. Please don't do that to Montell Jordan's song. That's a classic. Ha! I also love Cyndi Lauper, and The Notorious B.I.G., and oh! Yes. I've got a good one! 'No, I don't want no scrubs,'" she sang.

"'A scrub—'"

Jade's hand shot forward, palm up. "No! Please don't sing."

Nixon belted the rest of the line. The tune was way off. His voice cracked. Full-bodied laughter erupted before he could butcher another note.

Jade was bent over the table. Water filled the well of her eyes. Her breath ran short. "Stop. Don't ever do that again."

"I think that was kind of decent."

Jade stopped laughing, tossed him a sideways glance and broke out laughing again. Nixon joined her. They dug up a few more songs and artists from the eighties and nineties and talked about how their parents served as the influence for their love of music that came before their time. Jade explained how her dad would play rap music when her mother wasn't around. Her mother refused to indulge. They moved to other genres and connected on a higher level.

"I would never admit this to my father, but their music is better than ours." Jade took a bite of her flatbread.

"Yeah. Don't let them know you think that. Who are some of your favorite artists now?"

"I listen to everything, so I have a bunch. My cousin's music is great, of course."

"Your cousin?"

"Yeah. My cousin is Kendall Chandler."

"The pop artist?"

"Yep."

"That's nice." Nixon's nod was slow, showing he was impressed.

"It is."

Topics around music continued. They also shared their appreciation for jazz and greats like Nina Simone. Also due to the influence of their parents and grandparents.

"Her music was raw, real, sometimes dark. When you listen to her, it's like...you feel whatever she was feeling. Know what I mean?" Jade shook her head. Her face scrunched as if she was feeling something Nina Simone felt at that very moment. "And she was so...badass!"

"Yeah. My grandmother loved her. I remember going to her house. She'd walk around in her caftan, her 'fro pushed back by a headband as if she was giving the seventies a face-lift. She was the coolest. Grams would sit in her favorite recliner, smoke skinny cigarettes and sip on brown juice while she listened to her Nina Simone. Ha! That's what she'd call her liquor." Nixon drifted into a nostalgic place that put a smile on his lips. "Brown juice," he repeated, grinning. He mimicked his grandmother's voice. "Boy, don't touch Gram's brown juice. It'll put hair on your lil balls. You ain't ready for that." Nixon laughed at the memory.

Jade's laugh started as a gasp. She slapped her palm across her mouth but couldn't keep the laughter from spilling between her fingers. "Your grandma sounds like fun."

"She was. Feisty, brilliant, no-nonsense and made the meanest banana pudding you ever tasted." Nixon shook his head, chuckling again. He pulled himself from that place where fond memories of his beloved grandmother lived, and returned to the conversation before him.

"She's gone." Jade's comment was more matter-of-fact than curious.

"Yeah. Just last year." Silence fell between them. "Lung cancer." He answered the question he assumed she didn't want to ask.

Jade shook her head. "Those damn skinny cigarettes. I'm so sorry." Jade put a hand over his. That jolt was present, but less shocking. "Sounds like she was an incredible woman."

"She was." Nixon took a slow breath in and out. He sipped wine. "What brought you to the program?"

"My mentor." Jade inhaled. "It's time for me to blossom—to be known for more than just my last name."

Nixon nodded. "My company is sponsoring the program and was offered a slot to send one of their employees. They asked. I accepted." Nixon savored his sip of wine. "I'm glad I took them up on the opportunity."

"Me, too."

The mood had turned somber. This wasn't the road Nixon wanted to travel with Jade.

"Are you in a rush?" he asked. The fullness of his voice returned.

"Not really. I just hadn't planned on hanging out tonight."

"Can I take you to one more place? You can leave your car here. I'll drive."

Jade held her hands up and let them slap against the table. "Why not?"

"Good. Let's go." Nixon called the waiter over, left way more than the cost of their wine and tapas, and stood.

He took Jade by the hand and led her to his car. Once inside, he tuned to a nineties station on satellite radio. Nixon belted each song, lyric by lyric, enjoying how hard he made Jade cringe and laugh at the same time. On some songs, Jade joined in, not seeming to care about the way he bruised the notes. Together, they sang, rapped, tapped beats on the steering wheel and dashboard. The music was so loud the car thumped with the bass. Drivers stared their way at stoplights. They sang harder. The music carried them over the Long Island Expressway, through the Midtown Tunnel and down FDR Drive.

Nixon didn't want to exit the car when they reached their destination. They sat through another three songs before getting out. Singing with Jade made him feel as good as the savory wine had.

Nixon opened her door and offered his hand to help her out.

"Where are we going, Nixon?"

"Someplace you'll love. A place where people our age listen to the music our parents loved."

"Okay..."

"Trust me."

"I kind of have to now. My car is in Long Island. Lead the way, Mr. Gaines. I can't remember the last time I've been to a club."

Nixon smiled inside. They walked half a block on the west side of downtown Manhattan, where numbered avenues turned into names. Nixon led Jade through a dark door on the corner of Varick Street. They felt the music pump like a pulse the second they opened the door. Inside, the lighting was dim. On the wall opposite the door, the bar was illuminated in blue, green, red and purple hues. Bartenders dressed all in black almost faded into the backdrop as they poured drinks to the beat pulsating through the room.

"Want a drink?" Nixon shouted. His voice was snatched up by the loud music.

"What?" Jade yelled back.

"A drink." Nixon circled his fingers like he was holding a glass and tipped his empty hand toward his mouth.

Jade nodded. Nixon held her hand tightly as they squeezed through the thick crowd. The bartender held up a finger, acknowledging Nixon. He took orders from several other people standing around.

"Remember the Time" by Michael Jackson came on and Jade's mouth formed an O. "I love this song." Before Nixon could protest, Jade dragged him onto the dance floor.

Nixon and Jade moved to the music. What Nixon lacked vocally, he made up for in movement. He matched Jade step for step and beat for beat. Jade stopped dancing, reared her head back, stretched her eyes and nodded her approval. Nixon winked. Jade continued dancing, reenacting moves from the famed video. Nixon enjoyed watching her. The song changed. Prince came on next. They sang, danced and laughed. A while later, their clothes stuck to them as if sweat were glue.

The DJ slowed the tempo with "Breakin' My Heart" by Mint Condition. Nixon pulled Jade to him and mouthed "Pretty Brown Eyes." Their bodies touched as they swayed together. Nixon could feel the moisture on the back of Jade's shirt as he placed his hand right above her backside. At first their dance was playful, mimicking the way their parents boogied. They chuckled at that, but soon the mood turned from playful to sensual. Heat rose inside Nixon's core, making him sharply aware of the contrast of his inner warmth against his wet shirt and the cooling sweat.

Nixon didn't want to stop dancing. Jade felt good in his hands. She belonged there. He didn't know how he knew that or why he felt that. All he knew was that her being in his arms felt right. She could make him change his ways and run toward commitment instead of fleeing in the opposite direction.

Another love song played. Again, Nixon's core grew

a tick warmer. He needed to stop dancing or Jade would be able to feel how her body against his affected him. Nixon looked at his watch. Two hours had passed, feeling like no more than a half hour.

The time was reason enough to get Jade back to Long Island. Nixon led her off the dance floor and bought two bottles of water. Jade sat in the one seat available at the bar and Nixon stood close beside her. Too tired to shout, Nixon kept the conversation to a minimum. After finishing the water, they made their way back to the car.

"That was so much fun, Nixon. Thanks."

"I'm glad you had a good time."

"I had an amazing time. I haven't danced that much since my sister's wedding. What about you? Club much?"

Nixon thought a moment. It had been a long time for him, too. "It's been forever."

"Well, that was just what I needed—a break from the norm." Jade yawned.

Nixon was tired, too. The day had been full, starting with work and then their brainstorming meeting. He lowered the music enough to color the background and headed back to Long Island. By the time they reached the Williamsburg Bridge, Jade had begun a light snore. He looked down at her hand resting in her lap and felt the urge to hold it. Nixon didn't want to wake her. Most of all, he didn't want to offend her or possibly come off as creepy. One day, he'd get to hold her hand. This time, Nixon welcomed the thought instead of questioning where it came from.

Chapter 11

"Hello?" Jade croaked into the phone. She opened her eyes and then closed them immediately. The sun was still too much to bear.

"That's not your mother. That's a man!" Jewel cackled loudly. Clearly, she was thoroughly amused by the line she'd clipped from the Austin Powers movie.

"Shut up, silly! I'm just waking up."

"Obviously! I can't believe you're still in bed. It's after ten o'clock. I've been calling you since eight."

"It's that early?" Jade's eyes were still closed. "Hang up and call me back at a respectable hour, why don't you."

"Red wine, huh?"

"A few glasses. I feel like I need another few days of sleep."

"Ha! I figured as much when you didn't show up for hot yoga. You would have never survived. How was last night?"

Jade peeled her eyes open. "Last night."

"You texted that you were hanging with some friends in the city."

"Oh." Jade hadn't had that much wine, but she was good and tired. Yesterday had been a long day and sometimes the things she did when she was exhausted looked similar to the things she did when she was tipsy. She had wanted to spend time with Nixon alone and she was glad she had.

"Well?" Jewel said, bringing her back to the morning.

"Oh. It was fun. We went to some wine bar on Northern and then a lounge in the city." Jade kept her response simple—ambiguous. Jade climbed out of her high post bed and shuffled through her room, which was fit for a bold dignitary.

Above her bed on one of the gray walls were black script letters that read *The Queen Sleeps Here*. The one black accent wall sparkled. Silver glitter had been poured into the clear topcoat. A peacock-colored dresser stood tall and handsome against the black sparkly wall. Above that a colorful painting reflected many of the other bold hues around the room. The crystal chandelier in the center of the ceiling cast iridescent prisms across the walls and furniture day or night. Her home was as nontraditional as her wardrobe.

Jade relieved herself in the adjacent bathroom and shuffled right back to the bed without breaking her conversation with her sister. She'd explained that they weren't out long, but chose to stop by a lounge that played great old-school music.

"Sounds like you guys had a great time."

Jade didn't bother correcting Jewel or confirming that it had been more than just her and Nixon who'd hung out together.

"Yeah. Now I'm paying for it." Jade scooted until her back was flush against her velvety headboard, and pulled the comforter to her neck. "Now I don't want to get out of bed."

"But you have to—we have our sisters' brunch today."

Jade groaned. "That's today?"

"Yes, it is! And we absolutely have to go. This is the place that Dad was thinking about renting out for Mom's birthday brunch. He wants our review as soon as we get back."

"Oh. Yeah. That." Jade flung the covers aside. "I guess I need to get dressed."

"I can smell your cabernet morning breath from here."

"Shut up!" Jade laughed, shut her mouth and moaned. "It is pretty bad."

"Eww! Go brush your teeth and put on something cute. I'm meeting up with Sterling after, so I'm driving my own car. See you there. Noon. Sharp, little girl."

"Hey! You're not the boss of me."

"I was born before you, so that makes me the boss."

"And Chloe was born before you. I'm going to tell her you've been bossing me around."

"Go. Get. Dressed!"

Jade sat on the side of her bed, laughing at the long-time family joke about who was whose boss. She didn't feel like moving. Jade picked up her cell phone and realized she'd missed a bunch of calls and had tons of texts. She checked the calls first. Her mother. Father. Kendall. Jewel. Nixon. After seeing Nixon's name she looked up at her wall that resembled a starry night. He'd called. Something young, giddy and crush-like squiggled through her core.

Last night was fun. They'd connected, but boundaries needed to remain intact. She couldn't be distracted in this program.

Jade checked her texts. Mostly, they were from the same people. Not her mother. El Chandler wasn't a texter. She preferred to hear the voice of the person she spoke to—preferably in person.

Falling back on the bed, Jade stretched until every limb felt as if it had been elongated. She moaned with that stretch and then dragged herself to the walk-in closet. Originally, it was another bedroom, which she'd converted with custom-built cubbies for her shoes, shelving for purses and bars at varying heights for clothes. She grabbed a pair of cut-up jeans, a black sweater and thigh-high boots. On her way out she slapped several switches, shutting off the recessed lights around the perimeter and the chandelier hanging over the center unit with rows of slender, velvet-lined drawers for jewelry and lingerie—or pajamas. Jade wasn't exactly the lingerie type. She preferred footie pajamas in the winter and tanks and panties in the summer, if anything at all.

In the car, Jade called Nixon back.

"Hey." She didn't know why she felt shy, as if this were the "morning after." She hadn't done the walk of shame.

"Good morning, or wait… Yes, there's still a little bit of morning left."

"Just a little."

"You didn't text me when you got in."

"Oh!" She did remember him asking her to do that. "Sorry."

"I wanted to make sure you got in okay."

"Yeah. I did. I guess that's obvious now."

"Ha. Yes." Quiet settled in the middle of their conversation.

After a while, Jade said, "Thanks for a great time. I

liked both places." Jade rolled her eyes, but quickly returned them to the road before her. She meant to direct the conversation to its end. She should have said something like "Thanks for checking on me," or "Okay, have a good day."

"Anytime! I had a great time, too." Silence returned for several moments. "Are you busy tonight?"

No! "No big plans." Jade banged her hand against the steering wheel. Why wasn't her mouth cooperating?

"I have tickets to a neo-soul preview tonight. A friend is performing. Would you like to go?"

Jade huffed. "Nixon. I don't know about—"

"I have more than one ticket available. You can bring a friend. I'll leave them at the door for you." He told her the address.

Jade could actually hear her heart beating. She huffed again and finally said, "Sure. Thanks."

"They will be waiting for you at the door. I'm trying to help my friend promote. Hope to see you there." A few seconds later he said, "No pressure. Glad to know you got home safe. Have a great day."

Jade smiled as if he could see her.

Nixon ended the call without Jade officially saying goodbye. She didn't want to bring anyone. She didn't mind being just with Nixon, but being around him scared her. She had to focus on being a top-notch professional. Laser focus was necessary. Nixon made those lasers dull. Plus there was Mitch.

Jade groaned and drove the rest of the way to the restaurant to meet her sisters in silence.

Chapter 12

Jade went alone, driving into Manhattan mostly in silence. Thoughts were her company, many of them trained on Nixon. She needed to keep her walls erected somehow, but wasn't sure how to truly manage that. In sessions, she mastered avoidance, even though her eyes roamed in search of him constantly. Jade was discreet, or at least hoped she was. Even with that, there was always work to do and people around serving as distractions. When the distractions were gone, leaving just the two of them to fend for themselves in that magnetic field, that was when it was hard for her. She could easily come undone.

Jade's GPS told her that she'd arrived at her destination. She peered at the buildings lined up like uneven teeth, trying to spot the right one. The lounge had dark windows with the words *Juke Joint* playfully scrawled like script handwriting. With her arrival came second guesses. Maybe she should have brought Jewel with her, or even Serenity. Her soon-to-be sister-in-law loved music and played several instruments quite well herself. Serenity always introduced Jade to new artists and underground bands.

Jade wasn't ready to reveal herself to anyone when she was around Nixon—especially her sisters. They knew her too well. She'd introduce Nixon with all the nonchalance she could muster as some guy from her program. But they'd see right through that. Had Kendall been in New York, Jade definitely would have brought her. Kendall knew Jade's secrets and would surely carry them with her to heaven. According to the family tree, they were cousins, but to each other, they were the best of friends.

Jade drove around for a while in search of a parking spot. Finally, she pulled into a garage and handed her key over to the attendant. On the walk back to the lounge she dialed Kendall, but didn't get an answer. Jade felt like turning back. This wasn't a good idea. It felt like sticking a fork into an outlet. Eventually she'd get electrocuted.

At the door, Jade pasted a smile on her face and walked in with her head lifted and chest out. A beautiful full-bodied woman sat near the door, her head wrapped in a royal blue fabric, which matched her skirt. She smiled and cavernous dimples appeared in her cheeks. She had a warm vibe that immediately made Jade feel welcome. This woman was a Jill Scott reincarnation.

"Ticket?" the woman asked.

"Uh, one has been reserved for me. I was told it would be here at the door."

"Sure, honey." The woman's tone held a sweet lilt, reminding Jade of sweet tea and her great-aunts in the South. "What's your name, honey?"

"Jade. Jade Chandler."

The woman flipped through a few tickets, pulled out Jade's and presented it to her. "There's two here."

"Oh. My friend couldn't make it. I'll pay it forward."

"So nice of you. Enjoy the show, sweetie."

"Thanks." Jade took the ticket and headed past the nice woman with the sweet tone.

The lounge was full, but not packed to the hilt. Though she'd never been to a juke joint, Jade imagined that despite this establishment's modern flair, it captured the essence of a real juke joint. She loved the way the rough, sultry essence blended perfectly with modern furnishings. One wall was filled with signed pictures of celebrities and musical legends. The others held art, with the likenesses of people like Langston Hughes, Billie Holiday and B. B. King, and colorful abstract paintings. You could make out the presence of musical instruments if you studied it long enough. She spotted a picture of Nina Simone and smiled. Jade wondered how many people her age enjoyed Nina, and imagined that it wouldn't be many.

A stage was set up opposite the door, with instruments crowding the small space. Somehow Jade already knew she would enjoy herself even if she were alone.

Jade headed to the bar. The atmosphere called for a drink with a little more soul than a regular old glass of wine. Her eyes scanned the menu. No fried catfish for her tonight, though it sounded amazing and reminded her of her grandmother. She recognized some of the names of the drinks as songs from old greats. In honor of Nina, she ordered the Mississippi Goddam and chuckled.

When the bartender had handed her the drink, she turned and found Nixon walking toward her. At the sight of him, Jade gulped a sip and had to clear her throat. Nixon was a stunning man. His toned, tall frame looked scrumptious in the stylish shoes, jeans and button-down shirt. The buttons at the top were open, showing a simple chain and cross sparkling against his caramel skin. He smiled at her and she wanted to finish her drink in one large gulp, but resisted.

"Glad you made it." Nixon gently touched her arm, leaned over and kissed her cheek.

That spot tingled. Jade said, "Hey," but didn't move. She wasn't sure if it was the lighting, the atmosphere or the mischievous spirit of juke joints of the past coming to life, but she felt like knocking down the walls she'd carefully erected around herself and letting go.

"You look nice." Nixon smiled again.

Jade felt something in her gut flutter. *Forget Mississippi, Nina. Nixon Goddam.* She chuckled at her thought. "Thanks. You look rather nice yourself." She decided right then and there that this first drink would be her only one for the night. The lounge and Nixon were intoxicating enough.

Nixon looked beyond her on both sides. "Did you come alone?"

"Oh. Yes. Everyone else had commitments." She cleared her throat again after that little lie.

"I have a table reserved up front."

"Great! Lead the way."

Jade followed as they snaked through the crowd. She was glad she'd come, but worried about what this whole atmosphere was doing to her resolve. Was this what happened to people in real juke joints back in the day? Were they filled with wild inclinations to toss aside their inhibitions? What fun, indulgence, Jade thought. She already knew she would come back to this place sometime soon.

Jade used to hang out regularly. Now her friends and siblings preferred dinners and brunches. This place made her long for the days when she'd shed caution and hung long and hard, and then woke up with five ultrasensitive senses—eyes that couldn't bear light and a head that shunned the softest sounds. She'd promise never to hang out and drink again, but found herself back in the same clubs the very next weekend. Jade laughed. That was how she'd felt after the first time she hung out with Nixon. Both the cocktails and Nixon were intoxicating.

Like a gentleman, Nixon pulled out her chair. She sat right in front of the stage and Nixon took the seat next to her.

"I love this place." Jade looked around, taking it in a little more.

"It's pretty cool, isn't it?"

"And it has a…feel," she said, for lack of a better word.

Nixon smiled. "Yes. It does."

Jade raised a brow. There was something sultry in his simple response. Or was it the cocktail? She looked at her drink. It was now half-gone. Jade put the glass on the table. *Pace yourself.* She looked up at Nixon, catching him watching her. *With the drinks and with him.*

"What time does the show start?" she asked.

Nixon looked at his watch. "In about ten minutes." He nodded toward the small dance floor. "Wanna dance?"

"Let's go."

Nixon stood and reached for her. She took him by the hand and allowed him to lead her to the floor. A song from the seventies played. She didn't remember the name or artist, but she knew the words. It was one of her father's favorites.

For several songs, she and Nixon danced, teasing each other with their moves, playfully trying to outdo one another. They mimicked their parents' style of dancing and laughed hard, bending over to let the laughter spill unhindered. Eventually, a voice resonated from the stage, announcing the band for the night, and everyone made their way back to their seats.

A tall woman came out first, doing various renditions of popular neo-soul artists. Once she'd effectively warmed up the crowd, she exited with grace, to explosive applause. Jade was reminded of when Chloe would hit the stage and leave everyone within hearing mesmerized. Her sister was better, of course.

Moments later, the headliners came on. Nixon pointed out his friend, who was the pianist. He joined in with the lead singer for one of the songs. The deep timbre of his voice made her insides rumble. The group was amazing and ended their first set to more thunderous applause.

Jade turned to Nixon. "I'm really glad I came. Thanks for the invitation."

"You're an old soul like me. I had a feeling you'd enjoy it."

"Your friend was so good. How long have you known each other?"

"Since grade school. We grew up together. I try to support him whenever I can."

"That's great! We know some talented people."

"You have friends who sing? Oh, yeah. Your cousin is *the* Kendall Chandler!"

"And my sister is an amazing singer, too. My brother and his fiancée both play several instruments."

"Wow. Maybe I'll meet them one day." Nixon's smile made warmth spread in her belly.

Jade took that bait, tilting her head as she responded. "Maybe you will." She picked up her fresh drink and took a sip, peering at him over the rim of her glass.

"Are you flirting with me, Jade Chandler?"

"Maybe..." She kept her eyes on his.

"I'm pretty good at that myself."

"Not as good as me, I bet. And double entendres…" She waved dismissively. "I'm great at those, too."

"You're competitive."

"You could say that."

"Well, let's see how good you *really* are."

Jade accepted the challenge with pursed lips and a tilted head. "Oh, I'm very good…at what I do." Her shoulders lifted as she chuckled.

"I like good. I do a number of things well myself."

They went back and forth a few times with charged innuendos, until silent seconds passed as they tried to hold in their laughter. But then they failed, and muffled chuckles morphed into full-blown cackles. Their intended suggestive remarks were coming off more cheesy than sexy, more comical than sensual.

Jade shook her head and held up her hand, palm out. "Okay. No more. Please no more." The other hand held her belly.

"Those were pretty bad. I'm embarrassed." Nixon's head fell back and he let his laughter roar.

Tears from laughing filled Jade's eyes. "Oh my goodness." She flattened a hand against her chest. "That was hilarious!"

Their jesting died down just as the band was beginning their second set, which was even better than the first. Jade swayed to the music, caught up in the rhythm. Nixon bobbed his head and tapped his hands against the table. Several times they held each other's gaze or laughed, and bobbed their heads to the beat. Others ended with Jade feeling like Nixon was using his eyes to transport himself into her system. By the time the performance was over, Jade felt the full effect of Nixon. There was a lot to like about him and she loved when a man could make her laugh.

The applause died down as the band left the stage. Music filtered through the speakers. Chairs scraped against the floor. Some patrons took to the dance floor. Others headed to the bar, while quite a few made their exit. Nixon took Jade's hand and led her toward the back of the lounge, to a room where the band members were gathering their things.

"Lee!" Nixon called out.

"What's up, Nix?" The two embraced in a warm but masculine manner, ending with a strong pat on the back. "How did we do?"

Nixon looked at him as if his question was ridiculous. "Great! What do you think?"

"Good."

"I want you and the band to meet Jade. She's a friend of mine." Nixon presented her proudly.

"Hi! It's very nice to meet you."

"It's nice to meet you, too. I'm glad you could come and I hope you enjoyed the show."

"Oh, I enjoyed it!"

"Good." Lee took her to meet the rest of the band.

They chatted for a while before Nixon and Jade made their exit. He walked her to the parking garage and then waited with her while the valet retrieved her car. Nixon tipped the attendant for her.

"Let me take you to your vehicle," Jade offered. This was her way of getting a little more time with Nixon.

"Sure." He rounded the front of the car and hopped in the passenger side.

They said little as he directed her to where he'd parked. Though few words passed between them, the small space in the car was filled with so much more. The air crackled around them. The usual sizzle of their close proximity had become electrified. Sensual tension thickened the interior, warming Jade without any added heat from the vents.

By the time Jade pulled up beside his car, she knew she didn't want him to leave. For several moments neither of them moved. She cleared her throat. He cleared his.

"I had a great time. Thanks again for inviting me." She awkwardly pushed her words into the quiet.

"I'm glad you decided to come."

Jade focused on the tiny raindrops now falling on her windshield. "Me, too."

Again silence blanketed the interior of the car.

"Nixon."

"Jade."

They spoke each other's name at the same time. Both chuckled. Jade wanted to tell him they probably shouldn't continue hanging together, but didn't want to hear those words come from her mouth. They were approaching a slick slope. She could feel herself sliding right into his arms—perhaps even his bed.

Jade turned to face him. "I—" she started, but before she could say another word, his lips covered hers with warm deliciousness, swallowing her oncoming verbal protest.

She didn't resist at all. Jade had already imagined what those perfect lips would feel like. The real thing was way better than what she'd experienced in her daydreams.

Chapter 13

The passing days hadn't diminished the deliciousness of Jade's mouth on Nixon's. Visions of them dancing at the lounge and the feeling from that kiss in her car invaded his thoughts and lingered on his lips. He could still feel the moist softness. Traces of heat had consumed him the second their lips had connected. Their first kiss was cordial, as if they were carefully exploring new ground without disturbing the landscape. It left both of them breathless. The next kiss was deeper—greedier. They'd grappled with one another for more. More followed. More wasn't enough. Shielded by fogged windows, they'd stayed in the running car, trying to fill an insatiable well with the taste of each other.

Jade had not only filled his mind, but crept into his dreams. One was so erotic that Nixon woke up firm and grinning. What had she done to him? This was a first for Nixon. He questioned and liked it at the same time.

It was time for a real date. No more offers to casually "hang out." Their attraction for one another was clear. Undeniable—dangerously flammable. Nixon wasn't one to beat around the bush. And he wanted that date to be tonight. He couldn't wait another week.

Nixon thought another moment. He couldn't compromise her reputation in the program. Keeping his attraction at bay in session was key. A low profile was a must. Since they began spending time together, she avoided him in class even more. Avoidance became a game. Sometimes they'd pass slick, knowing smirks across the room. Nixon was fine with that, as long as he'd be able to make her his outside of their professional arena.

He needed to explore this thing he was feeling. Since Jade showed up in his life, he hadn't even thought about the other women he'd been seeing here and there, and didn't miss them when they didn't initiate a text or a call.

Nixon shifted his mind to his mother. He tapped his way through his phone icons until he arrived at her number, next to the name Queen.

"How's my favorite lady?"

"I'm glad I'm still your favorite!"

"You'll always be my favorite. What's up?"

"Work." His mother sighed.

"What's wrong, Ma?"

"Nothing," she said quickly, as if she'd been caught off guard. "Nothing's wrong, baby boy." She was Queen and he was Baby Boy. It didn't matter that he was a few years shy of thirty. Somehow he knew that even at a half century, he would still be her baby boy.

"It doesn't sound like *nothing* is wrong."

"How's work?"

"Fine. I have my class for the leadership program today."

"So you don't have to go into the office?"

"No. The class is a full-day session."

"Oh." She said nothing more for several moments. "Okay. I don't want to keep you and I do have to get to work. You're coming this weekend?"

"Wasn't planning on it, but I'll come on Sunday."

"That would be nice. I haven't had the pleasure of setting my eyes on your handsome face in a few weeks. I thought you'd forgotten about your mother. I'll make you some mac and cheese. Sound good?"

Nixon's brows rose and his mouth watered. "I could never forget about my beautiful mother or her mac and cheese. I'll definitely be there."

She chuckled. "Okay, see you Sunday. What time?"

"How about two o'clock?"

"Yay! Make it three. That way the mac and cheese will be piping hot. I'll make it fresh when I get out of service."

"That sounds perfect."

"Okay, baby boy. I need to get to work."

Nixon said goodbye, but several moments passed before she actually closed the connection. Nixon always waited for her to hang up first, to avoid ending the call before she was finished speaking. She usually had several "one-more-things" to express, and he never wanted to make the mistake of hanging up on her.

His mother's voice always held a cheerful air. Today, it sounded heavy. Something was troubling her. She never held back much from him, so he knew he'd find out soon. He'd make it a point to call her again after lunch. Right now he needed to get out the door in the next few minutes, if he was going to make it to his session on time.

Nixon's mind returned to Jade and warmth pooled in his groin. Standing in front of his full-length mirror, he assessed his attire. He'd taken special care, as he usually did on days when he knew he was going to see Jade. Today he wore his favorite navy blue suit, without a tie, and a crisp white shirt. He looked professional, though the suit was the most comfortable in his wardrobe.

Nixon's phone vibrated. The sound was muffled. He looked around, wondering where he'd left it, and spotted it among the ruffled covers on his bed. He quickly closed the space between the mirror and the bed. His mother could be calling back. Nixon grabbed the phone and swiped the screen before the ringtone stopped.

"Hello." He hadn't really paid attention to who was calling.

"Uh. Yeah. How are you doing, son?"

Nixon always tried not to flinch when his father called him *son*. "How can I help you, sir?" His tone was cordial. Tight.

"So formal? Heh." His father's chuckle was awkward. Nixon didn't bother to respond. No response was better than saying any of the words that swirled in his head. He wasn't fond of his old man, but disrespecting him would upset his mother. "I'd like to talk to you."

"About what?"

"Are you going by your mother's house this weekend?"

Nixon wondered if his mother had just told him that he was coming by. "Yes." He almost lied.

"Yeah. Okay. Good. I'll try to see you then."

Nixon snorted sarcastically. His father's "tries" had failed since he was a child. "Sure."

"Okay, son."

Nixon heaved a deep breath and let it out slowly. "Dad," he replied, with a dry curtness.

"Hope your day goes well."

"Thanks." Nixon ended the call and closed his eyes,

wanting to go back to the way he'd felt before his father's call.

Squeezing his eyes tighter, he conjured up an image of Jade, then opened his eyes and sighed.

Once he was in his car, he tapped the buttons until his radio erupted with laughter from Nixon's favorite comedy station. He needed laughter. Those jokes accompanied him all the way to the university where their sessions were held. Each joke eased his stiff shoulders a little more. Nixon hadn't realized how tightly set his jaw had become after speaking with his father. He realized it as he listened to the comedians. Laughter loosened that and his rigid back.

Walking into the conference room and seeing Jade's shapely frame from behind washed away the rest of his angst. What kind of woman could change a man's mood the instant he laid eyes on her?

"Good morning." Nixon greeted the members of his cohort as he headed toward his seat. After resting his binder on the table, he headed toward the coffeemaker, once Jade had filled her cup and moved away. For a brief second their eyes locked. He responded to Jade's slight smile with a discreet wink. She playfully rolled her eyes and made her way to her seat. Nixon tried to take his eyes off her, but couldn't. He'd watched her a bit too long. If that continued, someone was bound to notice.

"I guess I'd have to admit she does look nice in that outfit."

Nixon whipped around to find Julia standing close enough for him to feel the current of her static cling. "Good morning, Julia." He hoped she hadn't caught the wink.

"Good morning, Nixon," she sang, twisting her body seductively.

Cleavage bubbled out of the center of her low-cut shirt. Careful not to appear inappropriate, Nixon averted his eyes, but apparently not quickly enough. Julia lifted her ample bosom to offer a better view and giggled.

Nixon headed for the coffee. Julia followed. Again, she stood so close that he bumped her arm as he tried to pour a cup.

"Is she your type?"

Nixon smiled.

"What is your type, Nixon Gaines?"

Nixon thought for a moment. "The female kind."

Julia parked her hands on her hips and twisted her lips. "That was a cop-out."

Nixon grinned, tossed the stir stick in the garbage and headed back to his seat. He kept his eyes on the opposite side of the room to keep them from getting stuck on Jade again. Julia's comment about Jade looking nice in her outfit was a gross understatement. Nixon had never seen professional attire look so sexy on a woman before. Jade's skirt careened past her perfect curves and stopped just below her knees. It fitted as snugly as a mummy's bandages, but didn't appear inappropriate. The ruffles on her matching blue shirt gave her look a sweet feminine appeal. She had the air of a woman who knew how to handle business, while having the ability to snatch a man's breath at will. Her hair was pulled into her signature bun at the crown of her head. A few strands hung loosely, rebelling against its polished attempt, adding even more to her feminine appeal.

Between Jade's beauty taunting him and Julia's overbearing attention, it felt like they were the only three people in the room, until the facilitator greeted them collectively, calling everyone to order.

"Good morning!" The group responded in unison, before diving into the topic for the day and reviewing the status of each team's project.

The afternoon went by as fast as the morning. Nixon realized he hadn't asked Jade about her availability that night until minutes before the session ended for the day. He pulled out his phone, lowered it to his lap and texted about her plans for that evening.

He decided to have a little fun. His next text read: You're a great kisser.

Nixon watched Jade pick up her phone and discreetly read the text. A small smile creased her lips. He cleared his throat—his signal that he saw her smile.

Ha! Now? In the middle of class? she responded.

Trying to make up for the bad 1-liners from the other day.

Jade seemed to struggle to keep her grin behind tight lips. She texted three laughing emojis with streaming tears.

Nixon tapped out his next text: I want to take you out on a date. A real one.

She stretched her eyes wide.

Tonight, he added.

Her eyes widened even more.

Did you like the kiss? He was teasing her now.

Jade looked toward the ceiling. He watched her. Julia watched him.

Will you go out with me, Jade? Yes or no? Nixon added the checkmark emoji.

A small laugh escaped Jade's lips. Several eyes around the room landed on her. She coughed without looking up.

Okay. Yes, she finally responded.

Nixon texted five male dancing emojis. Be ready at 8.

Chapter 14

Nixon couldn't leave their class fast enough. He had a date to plan and a beautiful woman to impress. The second they were dismissed, both he and Jade departed with a general goodbye to the group and went their separate ways.

"Nixon!"

He had almost made it to his car when he heard Julia call his name. He paused before turning around and smiled. "Hey, Julia. What's up?" He hoped to come across friendly.

She jogged the rest of the way to him with her coat open despite the fall chill in the air. Her nipples pebbled against her silky shirt. Nixon tried not to, but couldn't help noticing her ample breasts bouncing and jiggling with each step. He turned slightly and jiggled his keys in his hand.

"Whew." Julia was out of breath. She touched his arm. "Want to grab a drink?"

"Thanks, Julia. That would have been nice but I have a commitment."

"Oh." Her shoulders fell. "Maybe another time." She sounded hopeful.

Nixon sighed inwardly. He had to make himself clear. Julia was a pretty woman—curvy and feminine. Sexy even. But Jade held his interest. He knew women well and his honesty could garner two responses: acceptance or bitterness. He thought about saying that he didn't mix business with pleasure, but that would be a bold-faced lie, especially when he was rushing home to prepare for a date with Jade.

"We should all go out for drinks the next time we get together to work on our project." He hoped she'd get his friendly drift.

"Oh. I was thinking just you and I."

"Julia…" He paused, carefully lining up the words in his head. "I just started seeing someone."

"Oh! Um. That's cool. It was just a friendly gesture. No problem. I guess I'll see you next week. Have a good weekend, Nixon." Julia paused between each sentence as if she had to think about what to say next. She turned and made a hasty exit.

Nixon didn't want to hurt her feelings, but had to let her know he wasn't interested. If Jade wasn't in this program, Julia would have stood a chance. But Jade… Just thinking her name made him aware of his own pulse.

Nixon made it home in no time. He set his phone to an R & B playlist and made a sandwich to ward off his hunger before dinner. The day had gone by without him making concrete plans for his date with Jade. She was a Chandler. How could he take a woman who presumably had everything on an impressive date? Nixon lowered the music and picked up his cell phone. His friend answered after three rings.

"What up, Nix?"

"It's all good, Jay!"

If anyone could give him a great idea about impressing women, it was his frat brother Jay. Romance wasn't Nixon's problem. He needed Jay's creative mind to help him think up a unique experience. A nice dinner wasn't going to cut it with Jade.

"Help me out, bro. I met a woman."

"Whoa! She must be special."

Nixon thought about the air when she was around. "Yes. She is. We've hung out a few times, but not like an official date or anything. That's tonight and I need some ideas."

"On Long Island or you're bringing her to the city?"

"Not sure yet."

"Okay. There's a great restaurant on—"

Nixon stopped Jay before he could finish. "That won't do. She's a Chandler, as in Chandler Foods."

Jay whistled. "How'd you manage that?"

"I can explain later. But think about how to impress a girl who probably has everything."

"That's easy."

Nixon twisted his lips. "Easy?"

"Expense won't mean anything to her, but experiences will. What's her personality like? Think of what she likes and use that as your starting point."

Jay had a point. His advice stirred a few thoughts as Nixon quietly gnawed on his bottom lip. "I got it!"

"What are you thinking about?"

"Music. She loves music. A big Nina Simone fan. Old-school music. I've got it. Thanks, man."

"Let me know how it goes."

"Will do. Talk to you later, man."

"And, Nix? Stop by the next time you come back up."

"For sure. Later."

Nixon had his idea. He wouldn't impress her with fancy meals, but he could certainly appeal to what tickled her fancy. Nixon got dressed, sprayed on a few squirts of cologne and texted Jade for her address.

Within twenty minutes, Nixon pulled off the Northern Parkway. A few lefts and rights later he landed on a dim winding road flanked by lush greenery. In the year that he'd been on Long Island, he hadn't seen this part of the region. Unlike his home and the others he'd rented out, these grand homes were set far from the side of the road, sitting proudly on hills or hidden behind a quarter mile or so of bushes and fences.

Finally, Nixon pulled into a driveway that seemed more like a private road. Jade's large colonial sat on an incline. Tall white columns rose on either side of her double doors. Two of his houses could fit in her home. The property surrounding the house seemed expansive in the moonlight.

Nixon rang the bell and tapped on the door. Moments later locks clicked and Jade emerged, looking sweeter and sexier than she had earlier that day. Her all-black attire gave her a bit of an edgy look. The peekaboo shoulders of her top highlighted her supple brown skin. Slim-fitting pants were tucked into knee-high boots with a slim heel. Nixon almost didn't want to leave. He could have stayed with her right there in her massive home.

"Hey!" Jade leaned forward and allowed Nixon to kiss her cheek. "Come on in and give me one moment and I'll be ready to go."

Nixon stepped in and scanned the well-decorated space, which was a direct extension of Jade's character.

The space was unconventional. Contemporary furniture was paired with antique pieces, warm woods with glass accents—an eclectic mix of high style and a cozy essence topped with a feminine touch, like the crystal buttons in the velour-tufted couch. Nixon had seen decor like this only in magazines.

Jade offered him water and disappeared for several moments. Soon they were in the car headed to Manhattan.

Jade gasped when he uncovered her eyes after entering their private suite in the karaoke bar.

"Oh my goodness!" She covered her mouth. "I've always wanted to come to one of these places." She scanned the textured walls, huge television, the karaoke equipment, high-backed leather benches and the delectable Asian-inspired spread on the table.

Nixon was impressed with himself. He'd managed to find one place that she hadn't been. He picked up the remote and flipped through the song choices, stopping on a party starter from the nineties. Jade grabbed the microphone from the table and began belting out the song. They didn't bother easing into their date. They simply jumped right in.

Their food cooled as they sang song after song, doing dances from long before their time. After a few Nina Simone cuts, Nixon pulled up a rap and R & B duet by a popular female artist and well-known rapper from their favorite old-school era. Jade sang the chorus and Nixon came in on the rap. Jade bent over laughing when he kept fumbling the words. She cackled until tears flooded her eyes.

"Pretty Brown Eyes" was Nixon's next choice. He serenaded Jade, albeit horribly, but sincerely. She swayed in his arms as he butchered the tune from start to finish.

Jade applauded when he was done, and Nixon kissed her lips. He set the karaoke to play "Adore" by the late Prince and again held her in his arms, hacking at the tune at first.

Nixon looked into Jade's doe eyes and lost himself. As if being drawn by some unseen force, he leaned in for another kiss. This one stirred the passion inside him. Nixon held her closer, tighter, and kissed her breath away. Jade's hands gently touched his face, cupped his cheeks and roamed his back. With her head against his chest, they caught their breath and swayed together—danced and held one another close. The air around them grew thicker. Nixon's senses awakened, making him keenly aware of the feel of her body against his. He felt the rhythm of her heartbeat.

They kissed again. This time the kiss was ripe with desire, setting their bodies ablaze. Both sets of hands explored the other's body in the dimly lit private room. The only light came from the large karaoke screen. Nixon pulled her close. He pressed himself against her. He hardened against her. She ground against his rigidness. They teased one another's desires for several songs. He pulled away, panting. Casting a wanton look at him, she pulled him back toward her.

Rising to her toes, she whispered in his ear. "Let's get out of here."

Chapter 15

Nixon reached Jade's home in record time. The ride back from the city had been a sensual sparring. They held hands, kissed at stoplights and exchanged sexy innuendos. They shared goals, desires, and played games, starting with Name That Tune. Jade could hardly make out any song that Nixon tried to sing, since he was so bad at holding notes. He guessed all her songs. Next they played a game inquiring about their preferences in an effort to know each other better.

"Morning person or night owl?" he asked.

"I'm definitely a woman of the night," Jade joked with a naughty smile.

Nixon widened his eyes and then winked.

"Chocolate or vanilla?" she asked.

"Chocolate all day," Nixon said and licked his lips. Jade felt a clenching in her core at his response.

"Bucket-list wishes." She changed the game.

"You start," Nixon said.

"I want to jump out of an airplane," Jade said. "Now you?"

"I've never been horseback riding."

"Really! We have to fix that."

This continued to her front door. Inside they tried to keep their desire at bay, starting in her family room listening to old music and swapping childhood funnies. Between stories, there was laughter, kisses, touches, jokes and more sizzling caresses. The ability to hold out ran its course. Banter was swallowed by deep kisses. Their lips became magnets, unable to be separated. Jade slid her hands under Nixon's shirt. Felt his taut chest and dug her nails in lightly. She lifted his shirt to see his chest in the moonlight shining through the wall of windows flanking her fireplace. Jade's mouth watered at the smooth skin. She pushed his shirt higher, bunching it under his neck.

Nixon caught her wrists with his hands. "Are you sure?"

Jade looked directly into his eyes, licked her lips, took his hand and led him to her winding staircase.

Nixon swept Jade off her feet and carried her up the steps. She threw her arms around his neck and giggled. At the top she pointed toward her room. Gently, Nixon laid her across the bed. The moonlight found them again. They searched one another's eyes for approval one last time, finding it in a shared hungry gaze.

Jade pulled Nixon's shirt over his head and unbuckled his belt. He kissed her delicately, laid her back and explored every inch of her with his warm tongue. Jade burned with desire, while the moisture of his mouth put out mini fires along her skin. When he reached the folds of her center, her breath hitched, eyes closed and mouth fell agape. Nixon teased her bud, flicking, suck-

ing and then plunging his rolled tongue into her warmth.
He pulled back and blew on her, before capturing her
bud once again. The juxtaposition of the coolness of his
breath and the heat of his tongue nearly drove her insane.

Nixon suctioned her firmly but gently. Jade beat the
bed with her fists. He tantalized her in a pattern. First he
flicked, licked, sucked, and flattened his tongue against
her heat, then repeated each action. Side to side, Jade's
head shook vigorously. She couldn't decide what gave
her more pleasure. Yet each repetition took her higher.
Made her lighter until she felt like she was floating. Her
core clenched. With each brush of Nixon's tongue her
bud became more sensitive. Soon she could no longer
stand his touch. Jade squirmed. Nixon wrapped his arms
around her thighs and pulled her closer. Groans rolled
in her throat. Nixon worked her until she exploded with
pleasure. Her body trembled uncontrollably. She sang
her joy in sensual moans.

Nixon lifted his mouth to hers and let her taste herself.
Passion rumbled between them. Pulling back, he stared
directly into her eyes, sheathed himself and slid inside
her moist folds. Jade's eyes rolled back. She couldn't help
it. The pleasure was too intense. When she looked up,
Nixon's back was arched, his eyes closed and he looked
to be in delicious pain. They rose and fell together, creating a delectable rhythm. Their tempo began with a steady
climb and swelled into a ravenous thumping. Nixon soon
added bass, grunting with each delightful stroke in perfect timing with her panting. His grunts strung together
into one long, low, guttural moan. They harmonized,
slamming against one another, no longer in control of
their faculties. Ecstasy took the reins and propelled them
over the edge. Bodies quaked, trembled, shook. Muscles
clamped as powerful waves of pleasure roared through

them before leaving both limp and spent. Jade licked her lips. He was better than what her dream presented.

Jade caught her breath and rolled onto her side. Nixon lay splayed on his back, eyes closed as a smile played on his lips.

Jade asked, "You okay?"

"Couldn't possibly be better." Nixon propped himself on his elbow and faced Jade. "What about you?"

"Couldn't possibly be better." Jade chuckled.

"This is going to make ignoring each other in class even harder."

"Ha! I know." Jade felt like the lucky girl in school. The most popular boy had eyes for her. She snickered inwardly.

Nixon traced a gentle line from Jade's forehead to her lips. "You're beautiful."

Jade kissed Nixon's finger lingering on her lips. "Thank you."

Nixon shifted in bed. "What else should I know about you?"

"What do you want to know?"

"Everything."

Jade couldn't help but smile. She'd gotten used to the electricity that sizzled across her skin when Nixon touched her. The man that arrested her attention the night of the reception was now lying in her bed. Avoiding him was a struggle, and the moment she'd relented to the constant tug of his presence, everything felt right. Jade wasn't a hopeless romantic, but something about Nixon made her want to be swept off her feet and carried off in his arms like the end of one of those old romance novels she used to steal from her aunt Ava Rae when she was younger. Everything that had anything to do with Nixon felt right. Being next to him in bed felt right. She felt like her connection with Nixon was already about much more than feeding one another's lustful desires. There was nothing casual about what they'd just shared.

After a great romp, Jade was usually ready for a good nap. But the man that stopped her from thinking straight for the last several weeks wanted to know everything about her and she was ready to reveal it all.

"Everything, huh?"

"Yes."

"Where do I start?" Jade cast her eyes toward the ceiling.

"From the beginning?"

For the next few hours, Jade and Nixon shared stories, from their earliest memories to when they'd first laid eyes on each other. Between tales, they kissed, made love and recovered in each other's arms. Nixon spoke little of his father and what he did say wasn't expressed with any warmth. Jade could tell there was much left unsaid. She didn't press him. There would be another time for that.

Jade's eyes fluttered against the glare of the morning sun. She woke to the weight of Nixon's strong arm over her body. A smile eased across her lips. Slowly, she lifted Nixon's arm, sliding from under it to quietly exit the bed. Jade tiptoed toward her bedroom door to retrieve her robe and cover her nakedness.

"Good morning." Nixon's usually deep voice was raspy.

"Hey. Good morning." Jade slid her arms into the silky sleeves of her robe and tied it.

Nixon sat up and looked around. "What time is it?"

"Just after nine."

"What time did we fall asleep?"

"No idea. I think a sliver of sun had just begun to

make an appearance before I drifted off. I can't be sure, though. I can't remember the last time I talked through the entire night—among other things."

"Neither can I." Nixon swung his muscular legs over the side of the bed. "I'll hurry and get out of your way."

"No need to rush." Jade almost couldn't believe she'd said that. Not many men made it inside her home, and those who did she had never allowed to linger. But she wasn't ready for Nixon to go. "Can you cook?"

"I was preparing Thanksgiving meals from the time I was a teen."

Jade looked at him and opened her eyes wide. "Impressive!"

"Love to see what we could cook up together in the kitchen." Nixon winked.

Chapter 16

The weekend was more than Nixon had imagined. Their Friday night date lasted until he went to his mother's on Sunday afternoon. He wasn't surprised that his father hadn't shown up, but he tried not to think about it. Saturday, Jade and he cooked together, exacting a rhythm in the kitchen that made it seem like they'd been cooking together for years. They simply fit. Nixon no longer questioned or challenged Jade's intangible draw—that it was still inexplicable. He'd gotten to know much more about that woman he'd felt an immediate connection to, and liked—no, loved—what he'd come to know. Jade's passion for life and her family, her intelligence and her witty manner made her even more beautiful to him.

Their nights were filled with sensual bouts of sleeplessness. They wore one another out. Nixon was going to have to pace himself with Jade. He'd never met a woman whose sexual vigor matched his. Nixon finally made it home late Sunday evening just to rest. Still he hadn't had enough of Jade Chandler.

Even as Nixon prepared for work, he couldn't erase delectable thoughts of their weekend together from his mind. Everything about their time together was spectacular, the laughter, the bonding, the deep reflective conversations and, of course, the sex. Nixon must have worn his joy like a cloak because a coworker eyed him suspiciously as he made his way to his office. Once inside, she showed up at his door.

"It seems somebody had a great weekend," the redhead teased.

A Cheshire grin played on his lips and he shook his head at her. Nixon wasn't going to give his coworker's curiosity the satisfaction.

The woman gave him a sideways glance and wagged her finger. "It's written all over your face. You don't have to say a word." She exited as easily as she'd arrived.

Nixon found himself humming as he fired up his computer. He paused and then laughed, realizing that his joy was much more evident than he'd realized. Shaking off the thoughts that came up with the memory of Jade, Nixon poured himself into his work as fully as he could manage.

"Nixon!"

He looked at Alex entering his office.

"Alex." Nixon greeted him without his usual formalities.

Alex nodded his approval. He'd told Nixon to stop addressing him so formally a long time ago. "How's it going?" Alex invited himself to the chair in front of Nixon's desk.

"Well. Very well."

"The program?"

"Great! I'm getting a lot out of it."

"And Ms. Chandler."

Nixon's smile slowly fell. He maintained a professional expression. "What about Ms. Chandler? I recall you asking about her before." For a moment, Nixon felt like Alex may have known about them, but dismissed that thought. How could anyone know? Besides going out at night, Nixon and Jade barely spoke in public.

"Any more thoughts about joining Mergers and Acquisitions? The department would benefit from your skills."

"I'm definitely still open to it and ready to talk whenever you are."

Alex nodded. "I understand that Ms. Chandler works on the foundation side of Chandler Foods. Do you know how involved she is with the corporation side?"

"Not really." Nixon was truthful and torn.

"Would you mind getting to know her a little more?" Nixon coughed. *Is this a game?*

"That's an interesting question. Why would you ask?"

"I'll keep it straight with you. Chandler Foods is producing billion-dollar brands and have gotten the attention of several consumer goods companies, including ours. I believe with the right offer, a merger or acquisition would be ideal. Timing is ideal, and if you have a connection, that could be an in."

Had this been another company, Nixon would have been excited about this news and ready to make a name for himself with any efforts he could contribute. Instead he felt like he could be in a position to betray Jade and didn't want that at all. They'd spoken extensively about work and it was evident that she was proud of what her family had been able to accomplish. He had no idea where they stood as far as acquisitions, but his gut told him they probably wouldn't invite it. Jade spoke of how important it was for her father to build that company and create a legacy for their family that honored his parents, who inspired the recipes that Chandler Foods was so famous for.

"Truthfully, sir, I don't know much about the company. We haven't spoken much during sessions. And the little I do know about the business is mostly what she deals with on the foundation side. Not sure I could be of much help here."

"Sure you can." Alex tossed him a dismissive wave. "Just find out more. We've done our research, but it's always good to have additional information that could potentially help seal deals. Engage her. See what she reveals about the company." Alex pressed his palms into the arms of the chair and lifted himself. "Looking forward to hearing what you find out. Never know what bits of information will be helpful in these endeavors." Alex headed for the door, then paused and turned back to Nixon. "Check in with my secretary and get on my calendar for dinner soon. We can kill two birds, talk about you joining our team and find out any information you were able to gather about Chandler Food Corp. Good day to you, Nixon." Alex was gone.

When Nixon was sure Alex was out of sight and earshot, he flopped back and huffed. Either way this went, it wasn't going to look good for Nixon. This was a prime example of why it wasn't wise to mix business with pleasure.

Chapter 17

The week flew by and Jade couldn't believe it was time for their weekly leadership session once again. Before heading over, she had to stop by her office. The staff planned a surprise farewell breakfast to send their program director off. Sandy outright refused to allow them to plan any kind of going-away party, period. They'd decided a simple breakfast would have to do because there was no way they would let her leave without doing something after all Sandy had put into the foundation.

Over the past several weeks, Sandy had spent most of her time traveling back and forth between her mother's bedside and the office. She prolonged her stay at the Chandler Foundation while they tried to find a replacement. It was important for her to help the new person get acclimated. Unfortunately, the right candidate had yet to come along and Sandy's mother was becoming more and more frail by the day.

Jade had been wiping tears since she woke up. By the time she got to the office, she gave up that futile effort and just let the tears fall. Her ache wasn't just for the fact that Sandy was leaving, but for all that Sandy had to bear. Jade hated to see such a selfless and kind person deal with such circumstances. Jade couldn't fathom having to witness her mother wither away, and imagined how much strength it took.

Jade arrived at work before everyone else and closed herself inside her office. Warm tears filled the well of her eyes again when she thought of how much she'd miss Sandy. Her staff was like family, and to Jade, family was the world. The bright spot of her week was all the time she and Nixon had begun to spend together.

Jade couldn't wait to get to her session later and have fun avoiding him due to all the new secrets they harbored. Nixon made love to her in a way that seemed possible only in a romance book. His style was passionate, attentive and skilled, and it caused her to quiver in places she hadn't realized were capable of tremors.

A knock on Jade's office door brought her back to the present.

"Hey." Her assistant's voice was somber.

"Hey," Jade replied. They exchanged sad smiles. Jade rounded her desk and the two of them fell into each other's arms and cried more.

"We have to get this place together before she gets here."

"Yes," Jade agreed. "Let's get started."

The two of them pulled out the decorations they had hidden in the storage closet and set up the conference room. Sandy loved flowers, so they'd ordered a grand bouquet as part of the decorations. A few other staff members joined them at this early hour to help out. By nine o'clock, breakfast had arrived and the setup was complete. Everyone took their places at their desks to mimic any other business day.

When Sandy arrived, Jade could tell by her red-rimmed eyes that she'd been crying, as well. That was all it took to start Jade's tears flowing again.

"Good morning!" Jade tried to sound cheerful when Sandy leaned on her door frame.

Sandy took in a long breath and released it slowly as she shook her head.

Jade stood from her chair, met Sandy at the door and hugged her neck.

"I so admire you for your strength," she said as she squeezed Sandy.

"I'm going to miss this place."

"We'll be here. Visit anytime you can. If you ever make it back to Long Island, a job will be waiting for you."

"You're the best boss lady a woman could ever have. And an amazing friend."

"Come." Jade took Sandy by the hand and led her toward the conference room. "I'd like to see everyone in the conference room now, please."

As planned, everyone looked surprised and confused, as if they had no idea why Jade was calling this impromptu "meeting."

"Everything okay, boss lady?" one person called out over their cubicle.

"Be right in," another called.

Jade slowed a little so they could reach the conference room before her and Sandy. Once they stepped aside, the staff yelled, "Bon voyage."

Sandy gave Jade a playfully narrowed sideways glare,

propped her hands on her hips and shook her head. "You guys! I said no parties!"

"This isn't a party. It's breakfast," Jade said. "Aren't you hungry? I know I am."

Everyone laughed. Other staff members led Sandy to the chair they'd decorated for her, and made her sit. Others served her breakfast. After eating, they presented Sandy with a plaque for her dedication to the mission, and parting gifts. Each person took several moments sharing stories about his or her experience with Sandy over the years. The gathering ended with a group hug, selfies and a few pictures of the entire staff.

Jade surprised them all by giving them the rest of the day off when she thanked her staff. "Have a great weekend and I will see you all on Monday. With one person down, it will be all hands on deck, so rest up. And remember, you're all the best ever!"

Jade smiled as she looked over the shocked faces. Mouths hung agape and eyes stretched in disbelief.

"Really?"

"Yes, really. Now let's clean up and get out of here. Sandy has a plane to catch this afternoon."

Jade didn't have to speak twice. A short while later, the conference room was clean and the office emptied out.

In the car, on her way to the session, Jade thought about Nixon and all the delicious nights they'd shared together. She couldn't wait to see him in the office. Their subtle flirtation was an exciting game. Jade was ready to play. Nixon brought a different element of excitement to her life and she loved it. She enjoyed letting things between them flow. Actually, she tried not to let her feelings get away from her. Nixon had a way of creeping into her system. The fact that she was thinking of him so much and desired his presence made her woozy. Usually, she prided herself for being able to keep it cool. Nixon made that talent disappear. He was like sugar—sweet, addictive and easy to overindulge in. Jade didn't want to get her feelings hurt, so she forced herself to keep her emotions under control. No man had ever challenged her resolve this way.

Nixon was incredibly handsome, fun, accomplished and a true go-getter. He didn't come with the pedigree that her mother preferred, but she knew her dad would respect him for his business sense and the way he carved out a successful existence for himself despite humble beginnings. The ideas he came up with for their business project were always well thought out and quite brilliant. She could see her and Nixon becoming a serious item. If things went that way, she wouldn't fight it the way she usually did. What if Nixon felt the same? That thought made her smile.

Jade shook her head. She had more to think about than Nixon. Her college buddy Reese Carrington was getting married and her bridal shower was coming up over the weekend. Jade hadn't had time to shop for a gift. Sandy was gone and it was one of the most critical times of the year for the foundation. In several weeks, their holiday ball was happening. The benefit was a huge undertaking and now they were going to be short-staffed. With all the work that had to go into preparing for the benefit, none of it included their regular operations and end-of-the-year responsibilities. The group project for the leadership academy was in full swing, taking up much of her spare time meeting with the team and doing research. And then there was the three-day conference that marked the culmination of the leadership academy, where they would meet other leaders from across the country and present their final business projects before judges. All of this would be added to any contribution she provided to the family's usual holiday gatherings. She loved her family traditions but was having difficulty seeing how she was going to get everything done. Mentally, she tried to categorize her to-do list.

Jade's thoughts carried her all the way to the program site, making her trip seem shorter. Slapping down her visor, Jade looked in the mirror, refreshed her lipstick, wiped the small smudge on the outside of her lip, smoothed her brows and exited the car. Her phone rang.

"Hey, Daddy."

"Hey, honey."

"To what do I owe such an early call?"

"I need a reason to call my baby girl?" Bobby Dale Chandler tried to sound offended.

"Of course not." Jade chuckled.

"Good. Listen." Jade noticed that Bobby Dale's voice turned serious. She pressed the phone close to her ear to make sure she caught every word despite the brisk winds whirling around her. "Do you have someone in the program that works for Wakeman Foods?"

Jade thought for a moment. "Oh. Yes. Nixon Gaines. Why?" Just saying his name brought a smile to her face and made her cheeks burn.

"Uh-huh."

Jade didn't like the sound of her father's response. "Is something wrong?"

"Has this Mr. Gaines—" Bobby Dale spit his name as if it were tasteless "—asked you anything about the company?"

Jade thought about all the times they talked about work and family, their professional and personal lives. She knew as much about Wakeman Foods as Nixon must have known about Chandler Foods. Had she shared something she shouldn't have? How did her dad know about him? "I guess."

"Somehow they are under the impression that we're interested in being acquired. I know how they operate. Watch this Mr. Gaines. In fact, just keep your distance."

Jade's mouth opened and wouldn't close. She couldn't even respond to her father. After a few moments slipped by with her suspended in awe, her dad finally bade her a great day, blew a smacking kiss through the phone and said goodbye.

Chapter 18

A sliver of trepidation rode Nixon's spine when he saw Jade walk through the door. Alex's last visit to his office raced to the forefront of his mind. Nixon went from enjoying every second in Jade's presence, and tasty thoughts in her absence, to wondering what it would be like when he saw her again after Alex's interrogation. They were getting closer and his feelings for her grew deeper with every conversation and intimate caress. But now Alex had put him on notice. They expected whatever kind of intelligence they could gain on Jade and Chandler Food Corp, and had put him right in the center of it all. He felt like a traitor. Somehow he was going to have to work his way around those feelings and be normal for the day's sessions. How would he manage that?

Usually their sessions started with Jade and him sharing knowing glances and sexy smirks as they playfully avoided one another, risking the possibility of getting caught gazing. That had become such indulgent fun. Once they left their sessions, they'd hurry to one of their houses to put out the fires they'd fanned all day. Today was different.

Nixon put on his game face, ready to swap sensual gazes, but found the usual light in Jade's eyes gone. She didn't glance at him the way girls do when they're crushing on boys. Instead, blank eyes and a stoic expression stared back at him. Nixon felt as if he'd run into a wall. Furrowing his brows, he questioned her reaction in silence. She cleared her throat and swallowed. Nixon wasn't close enough to hear the gruff sound, but he knew Jade well enough and he'd seen the shift in her throat many times before. She walked to her seat, put down her coat and headed to where the coffee and bagels were set up without saying a single word.

What had happened? Not wanting to make a scene, Nixon picked up his phone and texted Jade. Are you okay?

Nixon placed his phone facedown on the table. Jade sat right next to him, so there was no way she could completely avoid him. He watched her look at the phone and sigh. She didn't respond to the text. Instead, she looked at him briefly, frowned and averted her eyes.

Something inexplicable swirled in his chest. He wanted to know what troubled her and he didn't want to wait until the end of the day. A part of him thought it best to just let her be. If she didn't talk to him, he wouldn't have anything to report back to Alex and his team. Having her so close, yet seemingly untouchable, made him want to leave and not come back for the rest of the day.

Everyone chatted over breakfast except Jade and him. Both kept to themselves until Julia showed up at his side.

"You're awfully quiet today." Julia spoke to him, but her eyes were on Jade.

"I'm a little tired."

"Oh, is that it?"

Her skeptical tone annoyed him. "Yes. That's it."

Julia held her hands up in surrender. "Okay. If you say so."

Nixon exhaled. "I'm sorry." He hadn't meant to snap at her.

"No worries. I see you need space today. You're entitled." Julia frowned and walked away.

The morning dragged. Nixon struggled to maintain focus. Jade still hadn't responded to his text. She was right next to him.

When they broke for lunch, he leaned toward her and whispered, "Let's talk." He walked out into the courtyard. She followed him to the end farthest from the building.

"What's up?" he asked.

"Is your company trying to take over my family's business?"

Nixon's mouth opened, but no words came out—only a heavy breath. "Yes."

Jade's mouth dropped. "Is that why—"

"No!" Nixon stopped her. "From the first day I laid eyes on you at that reception, I wanted to get to know you. I just found out about my company's interest in your family's company."

Jade opened her mouth, closed it and opened it again, but didn't speak. After a while she said, "But you are going to the merger department. They've been courting you. This is part of the—"

"Jade!" He stopped her again. "I wouldn't do that to you."

"My father called me this morning to tell me about it and told me to stay away from you."

Nixon reared his head back. Her words hit him like

an unexpected bat to the face. "Stay away from *me*?" He poked a finger into his own shoulder.

"Yes." She folded her arms across her chest.

Nixon was crushed. "How would he even know who I was?"

"He asked if anyone from Wakeman was in my program. I said that you were and he said I should stay away from you."

Nixon held his forehead in his hands. He walked in a circle and stopped in front of Jade. "You have to know that I wasn't trying to get to know you just to collect information about your company. I'm not like that. I…" Nixon clamped his mouth shut, realizing he was about to lay his true feelings on the line. It wasn't time for that. This was not the right scenario to tell her that he couldn't stop thinking about her. He couldn't say that he longed to smell the scent of her skin and hair when she wasn't around. Most of all, he couldn't *dare* say that he'd never felt this way for any other woman—not even his ex-fiancée. He was falling hard and fast, out of control as if plunging from a plane without a parachute. He closed his eyes and breathed in, held it for a moment and let the air out. "That is not who I am. I hope you know that."

Nixon looked toward the conference room and saw Julia staring at them through the window. Jade followed his line of sight. He knew that she'd seen Julia, too.

"Let's talk about this later." Jade didn't wait for an answer. She walked back to the building.

Nixon dropped his head and shook it. *At least she said later.*

Chapter 19

Jade wasn't sure what to believe, but she did know she missed being with Nixon after the session. They had gone their separate ways. When she got home, she didn't even feel like hanging with her girlfriends or sisters. Briefly, she spoke to Kendall on the phone and resorted to binge-watching a show on cable until she fell asleep. She woke in the morning feeling just as down as she had the night before.

Jade wanted to believe Nixon wasn't capable of being so duplicitous. She hadn't sensed that in his kisses. There was authenticity in the way he made love to her. He couldn't have faked that. But then again, people did that sort of thing all the time. Why hadn't she been more careful? This wouldn't be the first time someone tried to get to know her just because she was a Chandler.

Jade pushed the covers aside and sat up on the edge of her bed. She stretched her neck from one side to the other.

It ached from bad positioning. Standing, she yawned and stretched until she was on her toes and then shuffled to her adjoining bathroom. Jade stared at her swollen eyes in the mirror. Deep creases lined her lids. She'd slept hard but couldn't claim it as restful. Cold water on her puffy face and a long, soothing hot shower should help. Jade turned on the water and let steam fill the large space while she studied her closet for something to wear to her friend Reese's shower. It was a midday event and Jade would have just enough time to get dressed, find a gift and make it through the hour-long ride to Scarsdale in time for the festivities.

Energized from the long shower, Jade dressed quickly and headed to Tiffany's to find something fit for a princess bride. Reese's family shared a similar background to Jade's. She was fun, witty and charitable, but also a daddy's girl in the most spoiled possible way. On campus they accused her of bathing in money. Tiffany & Co. was the perfect spot for such a bride. Jade collected almost every piece of their travel collection and had them wrap it in a large box with their signature blue paper. Not bad for a last-minute gift, and she still managed to arrive on time.

Inside the banquet room at the country club, Jade wasn't surprised to see several other packages from Tiffany & Co., as well as other luxury brands. Reese would be elated. That stuff didn't matter to Jade. Reese's mother was worse than El, perhaps because she was born into her wealth while El and Bobby Dale created theirs. Mrs. Carrington held her nose higher than any woman Jade had ever known. Jade was afraid it would give her a permanent ache in her neck. Her icy exterior made many keep their distance. Under her pretentious disposition, she was a truly sweet woman who adored her only daughter.

"Oh! Jade!" Jade turned to find herself face-to-face

with Mrs. Carrington. "What a pleasure seeing you." She air-kissed both sides of Jade's face.

"Mrs. Carrington. You look amazing as always."

A stylish silk jumpsuit elegantly draped the woman's slim frame. Her face was tight from fresh nipping and tucking, but the looser skin of her neck revealed her years. Her ears and wrists dripped with gleaming diamonds. The ridiculously large rock on her ring finger looked like it was custom-made for Wilma Flintstone.

"I try, dear. Gotta keep the old man reminded of what he's got. Ha!" Mrs. Carrington threw her skinny neck back and laughed hard. "Now let me see you." She guided Jade in a circle, checking out her fuchsia dress. She looked at Jade from the side and winked her approval. "You never disappoint. How's your mother, dear?"

"Mom is great."

"Tell her I said hello. We should get together some-time."

"Yes. You should."

"She's coming!" someone yelled, and everyone hurried to the center of the room.

"Places, everyone." Mrs. Carrington clapped her hands without spilling the champagne she was holding.

The door to the beautiful sun-filled room swung open and Reese stood frozen, yet perfect in the center of the frame. Her left hand covered her gaping mouth while showing off her huge glistening diamond.

"You guys! You tricked me!" She looked back at the two girls behind her. Jade remembered them as Reese's childhood friends who'd visited their campus a few times during their college days.

Mrs. Carrington walked toward Reese with open arms, embracing and rocking her shocked daughter. When Reese pulled back, she wiped tears from her eyes. "Mother! You were in on this, too? Chastity lied and told me she wanted to look at this place for her parents' anniversary dinner. We're supposed to be on our way to brunch!" Reese playfully rolled her eyes at her friends, who only laughed in response.

Mrs. Carrington laughed, too. Reese looked past her mother and connected her eyes with Jade. "Oh my goodness. Jade! You're here." Reese wrapped her arms around Jade, almost tilting her toward the floor.

Jade hugged her back tightly. "I wouldn't have missed this for the world. I'm so happy to see you."

Reese stepped back and wiped more tears. Looking around, she noticed person after person she was surprised to see. After several more excited greetings, her two friends led her to the chair specially decorated for her. She sat, looked up, and her mouth dropped.

Jade looked in the direction that caused this second wave of shock and her eyes landed on Alyssa Chambers, the last third of their college trio. Jade, Reese and Alyssa were the best of friends during their four years of college and had done well with staying in touch, until Alyssa started taking assignments out of the country. They lost touch after that. Jade was as surprised as Reese when she saw Alyssa.

Jade and Reese looked at one another in disbelief and then looked back at Alyssa as if she was a mirage. The three ran toward each other, meeting in a haphazard group hug. Screaming, laughing and hugging, each looked the others over and they squealed, making everyone else in attendance smile.

"How long are you going to be here?" Jade asked.

Before she could answer, Reese said, "I can't believe you're here, period." She touched Alyssa's cheek as if she needed to feel her face to know she was real, and then bounced on her toes.

"I'm home for good." Jade's and Reese's eyes widened. "Look at us," Alyssa continued. "The trio is back together again. I'm so happy to see you two." She squeezed them in her arms once again.

Reese looked over at her two friends and her mother. "You ladies really outdid yourselves. Thank you so much."

"Time to party," Chastity, one of her friends, said.

Music filled the space as their meals were served. Jade and Alyssa sat together.

"Where were you last?" Jade said, slicing into a piece of grilled salmon.

"Running teaching programs for a nongovernmental organization right outside of Abu Dhabi."

"Wow! And before that?"

"Uganda. I ran a program placing teachers in schools across many third world and developing countries. Most of the area was really impoverished."

"Oh, like that company Teach the Globe."

"No-o-o!" Alyssa sang. "That's one of the those companies that place teachers in prestigious prep or boarding schools for the super rich, who don't want their kids mingling with the general population."

"Ha! You're so bad."

"And truthful," Alyssa laughed.

"What brings you home?"

Alyssa paused a moment. Jade sensed she was grappling with information that she wasn't ready to reveal now—if ever. "I just started craving home. I got back a week ago and my mother said Mrs. Carrington had been trying to reach me."

Jade shook her head. "Anything for her princess."

"I know. Remember she would come to school and take everyone shopping?"

"Oh my goodness, yes!"

"You and Reese were the rich ones. I wasn't used to that and couldn't believe the insane amount of money she'd spend on the three of us." There was a far-off look in Alyssa's eyes. She shook her head. "Those were the days."

"I know. So what are you going to do?"

Alyssa covered her mouth and finished chewing. "Nothing yet. I submitted a few résumés."

"To do what?"

"Program work in the nonprofit sector. I've been doing it for years now and love the work."

"You're kidding me!" Jade dropped her fork, causing it to clink against the plate.

"What?" Alyssa looked concerned.

"I'm looking for a program director for the foundation right now!"

"Work for you?" Alyssa scrunched her nose. "Of course I would! Ha!"

Jade laughed. "Alyssa!"

"I'd love to work for the Chandler Foundation. It's my dream to give away rich people's money!"

Both ladies fell into another fit of laughter.

"It's done! We're going to be working together! I can't believe this," Jade squealed.

"I know." They hugged.

"When can you start?"

"Yesterday! You owe me."

Jade's laugh was quick and sharp, making her cover her mouth to avoid spitting out her food. "How about Monday, silly?"

"Okay!"

The next few hours were filled with zany bridal shower games, hearty laughter and tons of oohs and aahs when Reese opened gifts. The college trio reconnected in a way that made the years that swelled between them seem to disappear. After the shower, they went back to Reese's house for drinks and more reminiscing that carried them well into the night.

Jade left Reese's house feeling happy but tired. In the car, she checked all the messages she'd missed while having so much fun. Nixon had called several times and left numerous texts. She still didn't know how to feel about the situation with him. Jade would figure that out before she called him back.

She jumped onto I-95 and headed back toward Long Island. An hour later, she arrived at home to find Nixon sitting on her porch with his head in his hands.

Chapter 20

"Nixon?"

He stood, stuffing his hands in his pockets. "Hey." Showing up at her house wasn't such a good idea. His issues were too deep to reveal to Jade so soon. It didn't matter that he felt close to her. Nixon decided he'd talk to her about their incident yesterday and be on his way.

"Everything okay?" She moved closer to him.

Nixon stood rigidly, trying not to allow her touch to make him shiver. Their misunderstanding hadn't changed the kinetic energy that transferred between them. "I'm fine. I hope you don't mind me stopping by. I tried to call you."

Jade looked down. "I know. I was at my friend's bridal shower."

"Okay. Sorry to bother you." He paused, searching for the right words. He wanted to leave but couldn't seem to move. "We didn't get to finish our conversation yesterday."

Both of them sighed.

"Yeah. That was concerning."

"Yes, it was. I have some integrity."

Jade groaned. "Let's talk inside." She opened her door, flicked on the lights, put her purse down and walked toward the kitchen.

Nixon was hesitant at first, but followed her through the wide corridor. As much as he'd been in her house lately, the divide from yesterday's squabble made him feel like a guest all over again.

"Coffee, tea, wine?"

"Anything stronger?"

Jade chuckled. "Whiskey."

Nixon's eyes widened. "You drink whiskey?"

"My dad always said they'll know you're drunk, not stupid." Jade shrugged. Nixon's mouth dropped a moment before both broke out laughing. "Only the best, though?"

Jade disappeared and came back with a premier bottle of an aged single malt scotch. Nixon recognized it as one the gentlemen in Mergers and Acquisitions drank often. A single shot in some establishments ran around a hundred fifty bucks. She pulled two snifters from the cabinet.

"On the rocks?"

"Neat," Nixon replied.

Jade put a few pieces of ice in a glass for herself and filled his halfway without ice and handed it to him. She walked to her sunroom and sat in a wing chair on one side of a bistro-sized table, gesturing for him to sit on the opposite side. Nixon looked around and admired how cozy the room felt. The space wasn't filled with furniture. Besides the chairs they sat in, facing the wall of windows, there was a couch covered in yellow velour with a soft blue throw tossed across the back. Large pillows were piled in one corner of the room. Nixon imagined they could be used to sit on. A treadmill stood in another corner next to a wicker basket with rolled yoga mats sticking out of it. The windows spanned from the ceiling to about a foot off the floor. Jade picked up one remote and powered the shades halfway down. With another, she dimmed the lights in the room, creating a cozy ambience. The black of the night outside made the window reflect like a mirror.

They sipped in silence for a while. Nixon enjoyed the slight burn as the scotch smoothly slid down his throat. He sat back and for the first time in the past thirty-six hours began to feel himself relax.

"Jade."

"I know."

"Good."

"My father's call alarmed me—especially when he said stay away."

"They want me to join Mergers and Acquisitions. I don't think it's for me." He sipped. Nixon had been thinking about their offer since the session the day before. He felt good about the partnerships he established in business development. They seemed mutually beneficial. He wasn't convinced he'd have the same feeling about the businesses they worked with over in Mergers and Acquisitions. He wasn't sure what that would mean for him at the company, since they'd spent so much investing in his leadership development, but he had to do what he felt good about, even if it meant sacrificing a lucrative opportunity and possibly burning a bridge. Taking over companies that didn't want to be taken over didn't feel good. He wasn't a bully.

"I believe you." Jade sipped, too, but kept her gaze straight ahead.

Quiet took over for several moments.

"Now what?" Nixon asked quietly.

Silence descended again.

"What really brought you by here tonight?"

Nixon's father's face appeared before him. He twisted his lips and drained his glass.

Jade tilted her head. "That bad, huh?"

Nixon took a deep breath instead of responding. Jade took his glass to the kitchen and poured more scotch. She came back with his glass and the bottle, placing both on the side of the table closest to him.

"Or do you want to lie on the couch?"

That made Nixon laugh. After taking a more civilized sip, he put his glass down and sat back.

"My family situation is not like yours."

"Uh-huh."

"My father wasn't always there. He didn't leave me with cool quotes and sayings. He just left me." Nixon felt the weight of his own words. Resisting the urge to take another sip so soon, he continued talking. He'd been taught that scotch was meant to be savored, not gulped, and it wasn't his deadbeat dad who'd told him that. "I was that excited kid waiting anxiously in the window for his dad to show up. He'd call and say he was coming to get me. Most of the time he never showed up." The words came out with less effort than he'd anticipated. Talking to Jade came easy. He kept going. "Sometimes I'd wait well into the night, falling asleep on the living room couch hoping he'd come late and wake me up."

Jade sighed but kept quiet.

"I thought I'd left that boy behind." Nixon pressed his lips together. His emotions threatened to get the best of him. Jade leaned over and rubbed his arm. "He's still doing it and that little boy still gets upset. He called me last week, asking to talk. Said he wanted to meet me at my mother's last weekend. She cooked for me." Nixon felt himself smile. His mother…

Jade gave him the space to feel what he needed to feel. The gentle touch of her hand was sufficient, letting him know she was there to listen.

"He didn't show—of course." He huffed. "He called today. The words we exchanged should never be used between a father and son." Nixon closed his eyes and breathed for a long time.

"It's because of his absence that I became so successful. I wanted to prove that I didn't need him. But for some reason, I still care." Now the words seemed thick in his mouth, almost choking him. Nixon felt the sting of tears but refused to let any fall.

He'd done it—unloaded his soul at Jade's feet. Why had he chosen her? He couldn't say, but it felt right.

Nixon let his head fall back against the chair and closed his eyes again. He felt Jade take his hand in hers. They stayed that way for a while.

Nixon turned toward her—found her eyes closed and her head back, too. "Jade." He spoke softly.

She lifted her head and looked at him. When their eyes connected, something shifted inside his core. "I would never betray you." Why had he said that?

"Somehow, I know that."

As if compelled by an invisible force, both of them stood. Jade came to him and laid her head on his chest. He rubbed her back. She laced her fingers between his, lifted his hand to her lips and gently kissed his knuckles. He felt another shift, this time in the center of his chest and groin.

By the hand, Jade led him up to her bedroom. Even though it was just the two of them in the house, she shut the door behind them, closing off the heaviness of what

Nixon had just laid out. That was downstairs. They were upstairs, where the air felt lighter. A sense of peace slowly replaced his angst. Jade stood on her toes and began kissing the rest away. Nixon pulled her in, squeezed her in his arms without letting their lips disconnect.

Nixon hugged her like he'd never hugged her or any other woman before. He hugged her with his soul. Nixon lifted Jade in his arms and carried her to the bed. They kissed forever, sucking on each other's tongue and lips, exploring their bodies through clothing. Nixon took his time, savoring her like the fine scotch. Eventually he peeled off her dress, carefully, as if harried movements might spoil the moment. Jade returned the gesture as gingerly as he'd handled her.

Nixon scanned her nude body in the sliver of moonlight, admiring how it illuminated her smooth skin. They locked eyes, stared at each other for some time. Nixon felt like he was falling into her, connecting in a way that could never be severed. He kissed her again. Slow and soft.

Nixon leaned toward his pants and handed her his protection. She thoroughly rolled it over his stiffness, held him and readied her hips. His mouth covered hers with all his heat and passion. At the same time he entered her. She hissed over his tongue. Long, strong, measured strokes filled her cushioned walls. She tightened herself against him. Nixon's eyes rolled back. He didn't know how much more he could take. Maintaining a slow tempo became a struggle. The feeling was too intense to keep his rhythm steady. Their voices expanded to sensual crescendos as they called out one another's name.

Steady strokes morphed into erratic plunges. They slammed against each other. Sweat dropped from his chin. His kissed her again, devouring her mouth. She grasped at his back. Moaned her pleasure. Her hands grabbed his bottom, pushing him deeper. Her back arched. Soft moans turned to cries and mutated into breathy grunts. Nixon couldn't tell if they came from him or her. The sound of their bodies slapping against each other added a drumbeat to the music bellowing from their throats. Nixon released the last bit of control he possessed. Jade cried out. At the erotic sound of her howl, Nixon let go, spilling into her. His body convulsed, arresting and releasing his core. Jade wrapped her arms around him and pulled him close. Turning sideways, they lay in one another's arms until they were able to breathe.

There would be no more fighting what he felt for her.

Chapter 21

Nixon stayed with Jade the remainder of the weekend. They did get out on Sunday for brunch. Finally, he left late that night. They didn't see much of each other during the week because both their workloads picked up drastically. Texts and calls kept the communication going, but was far from as satisfying as being with each other. They agreed to let whatever was happening between them blossom naturally and pinkie-promised not to fight it.

Alyssa started her tenure at the Chandler Foundation and proved to be a huge asset almost immediately. The staff loved her instantly. The holidays were approaching and the ball was the biggest thing on their to-do lists. Alyssa worked closely with the development team to figure out what the programming department needed to do in helping to prepare for the annual festivities.

Friday's weekly session of Jade and Nixon's leadership academy had returned to their normal sensual peekaboo game of avoidance. Julia seemed visibly disappointed that they were back to their old ways. Saturday morning arrived with Nixon and Jade tangled in his bedsheets.

Jade's phone rang. Giggling, she reached through the morning light to grab it. Nixon kissed her spine as she answered. Jade tried not to let her giggles seep into her greeting.

"Hey, Jewel." She pressed her lips together, suppressing moans and snickers.

"What's up, lil sis? Need me to bring anything for tonight?"

Jade sat up in Nixon's bed. He was still kissing her and had started to caress her breasts. "Tonight?"

"Don't tell me you forgot."

"Oh Lord." Jade slapped her hand across her forehead. "The slumber party!" Nixon scooted down on the bed, pulled the covers back and began a line of kisses along her thigh. Jade swallowed to keep from moaning.

"Yes, the slumber party. It's your turn to host. I hosted this summer and Chloe did the spring. It's your time, ladybug."

"It just slipped my mind. This week at work was absolutely crazy. I'll tell you all about it tonight." Nixon's mouth grazed her center. Jade instinctively parted her legs. "Don't worry. I'll be ready." His tongue flicked her center. A moan escaped. Jade threw her hand over her mouth.

"Hello?"

"Uh...nothing. See you later."

Jade ended the call before she gave herself up. She tossed the phone, grabbed a pillow and swatted Nixon, whose face was still between her legs. Nixon snatched the pillow, tossed it over the bed and pulled her center closer. Not resisting, Jade fell back against the headboard and let him take her to paradise. They pleasured each other over and over again until their stomachs grumbled.

"We need to eat!" Jade held her belly in response to her stomach's last protest.

"We already did and it was delicious!"

"Silly!" Jade shook her head. "Food." Nixon raised a brow. "With sustenance." A grin spread across his face. "The kind you chew, swallow and it keeps your stomach from sounding like there are monsters in there fighting."

"Ha!" Nixon stood and stretched, showing off all his naked glory. He held his hand out for her. Jade scooted to the edge of the bed and took his hand. He guided her up and wrapped his arms around her. "Let's go get us some food."

Jade went to grab the robe she'd left there.

"Uh, uh, uh!" Nixon wagged his finger. "No clothes allowed in my kitchen."

Jade grinned. Nixon had so many ways of making her feel sexy. "If you say so."

Together they headed to the kitchen, completely naked. Nixon set his phone to eighties pop and they danced around the pots and pans, teasing each other here and there. After plating their meal, they placed it on trays and returned to the bedroom.

Settling back against the headboard beside her, Nixon fed Jade a piece of bacon.

Jade rolled her eyes, savoring the flavor. "I swear everything is just better with bacon."

"And butter," Nixon added, and they both laughed.

"I'm glad we were able to get past that whole situation from last week."

"Me, too. And I let them know I wasn't interested in moving over to Mergers and Acquisitions. My boss wasn't looking forward to losing me, anyway."

"Good. I just hope this doesn't affect your future promotions or anything."

They settled into a companionable silence while they ate. Jade held a question back, but then decided to ask anyway. "How are things with your dad?"

"The same." Nixon's face held no expression. He obviously didn't want to talk about his dad.

Jade let it go. Family was too important. Somehow she had to help him find a way to work something out with his father. "What do you have to do today?" she asked.

"Besides you?" She gave him a side-eye. "I'm heading to Mount Vernon to help my mother take care of a few things around the house, collect rent from our property managers and a few individual tenants. Just some regular business stuff."

"How many places do you guys have?"

"Fifteen."

"Wow!"

"We weren't dirt poor, but we did struggle a bit. My mother did the best with what she had after my father abandoned us. In college I learned about real estate being one of the best ways to build wealth, so I decided that was one way I was going to make sure my mother and I never had to struggle again. I saved money and together we bought our first property during my last year of college. With the equity from that, we were able to buy our next. I work with our property manager in handling rent payments and repairs. I don't want my mother to have to deal with any of the burden of that stuff."

"You never cease to amaze me, Mr. Gaines." Jade smiled proudly. Her father would love Nixon—especially if he hadn't been from Wakeman Foods. Jade remembered her father's warning to keep her distance and kept her sigh inside.

"I'm just glad I was able to help make life more comfortable for her, since she sacrificed so much for me as a single mom."

"That's sweet." Nixon's words made Jade's heart smile. She felt warmth spread in her chest. "It's clear that you're a mama's boy."

"Proudly." He stuck his chest out. "That's one of my favorite ladies."

"Who are your other favorite ladies?" Jade tilted her head, awaiting his answer.

Nixon leaned over and kissed her lips softly. "You."

She smiled.

"Don't worry. My mother and I are close, but she's not the crazy type that believes no one is good enough for her son. You're going to like her a lot."

Jade stacked their empty plates on the tray and placed them on the night table beside the bed. She turned to Nixon. "So you want me to meet your mama?"

"Of course."

"Are you sure?"

"Why wouldn't I be?"

"I just…"

"You're just the perfect woman."

Jade opened her mouth and closed it. Flutters released in her stomach and she smiled.

Nixon winked at her and kissed her lips again.

"So we're an item, huh?" It was more of a statement than a question.

Nixon looked at her like she was crazy. "Where have you been?"

Jade burst out laughing. Nixon joined her.

"We're an item!" She nodded and declared it confidently.

"Only if you're cool with that," Nixon said.

"I'm very cool with that." Jade straddled him and kissed his face. "So…do we consummate this…thing?" She sent him a naughty glance.

"Hell yeah!" Nixon wrapped his arm around her, rolled her on the bed and kissed her everywhere, leading to another mind-blowing, body-shuddering escapade.

They couldn't seem to get their fill of one another. Every time they finished, they'd start all over again until time started to work against them.

"I need to get to Mount Vernon."

"And I need to go shopping and get ready for my slumber party."

"A slumber party? Interesting."

"My sisters and I started this a few years ago once we all moved out of our parents' home. We get together in pajamas, drink wine, talk crap and laugh our butts off. It ended up becoming the best way for us to really catch up on each other's lives, especially now that Chloe is married and Jewel is engaged. I can't wait for you to meet them."

"I can't wait to meet them, too." Nixon pushed back the covers, got up and headed for the adjoining bath. "Wanna join me?"

"Only if you behave. We have no more time to waste."

"I don't make promises that I'm not guaranteed to keep."

Jade joined him anyway. They washed one another, shared a few kisses and dressed.

"I'm planning a special night for us. This time we will be out of the bed, okay?" Nixon said as he leaned forward to kiss her.

Jade rose on her tippy toes. "I bet we will end up back in bed anyway." She giggled as they kissed goodbye.

Jade stopped at the grocery and wine store on her way

home. The fresh aroma of lemon-scented cleaner met her at the door. The house seemed brighter when the cleaning service came. By eight that evening, Jade had prepared pasta with a seafood scampi sauce, garlic bread and a mixed green salad with cranberries, walnuts and goat cheese. She slipped her legs into her Minnie Mouse pajamas just in time for Jewel and Chloe to show up.

"I brought dessert!" Chloe held a homemade fruit tart in her hand, bright and shiny with colorful fruit covered in a clear glaze.

"And of course I brought more wine!" Jewel danced through the door. "I'm hungry," she said, making her way to the kitchen. "What's on the menu?"

"Seafood scampi, greedy girl!" Jade replied, following along with Chloe.

"Mmm. Now, that's one thing you make really good, lil sis."

Jade wagged her finger, punctuating her point.

"I also have popcorn for the movie." Chloe plopped the bag in her hand on the counter and spread popcorn, chips, the fruit tart and M&M'S across the black granite. "What are we watching, anyway?"

"Can we figure that out after dinner? I'm starving!" Jewel peeled off her coat and carried it back to the closet in the foyer. She pranced back in her graphic tank that read No Coffee, No Talkie, and polka-dot fleece pants.

Chloe, the classic-styled sister, wore a black pajama set with a T-shirt that read Namaste Asleep, and jersey pants.

"Well then, let's eat!" Jade announced.

She made sure the food was good and hot. The girls served heaping plates, poured glasses of wine and made their way to the family room, where the fireplace crackled with the promise of coziness. Jewel lay across the chaise. Chloe took to the couch and Jade sat on the floor.

The TV played only as a backdrop for the slurping of pasta and the chatter of sisters.

Jade was dying to tell them about Nixon, but held off until she couldn't hold it any longer.

"Okay!" She crossed her legs and held her hands out in front of her. That caught Jewel and Chloe's full attention. "I have a new boo!"

"Wait! What?" Jewel asked.

"Really!" Chloe sang, then smiled. "Who is he?"

"What does he look like?" Jewel countered.

"What's his name?" Chloe asked.

"Have you slept with him? Was it good?" Jewel asked.

The sisters tossed questions at her like darts. "Wait! One at a time? He's from my leadership program. He's gorgeous." She rolled her eyes for effect. "His name is Nixon. And yes… I've slept with him and he is A-mazing in bed."

Like teenagers, the three of them squealed.

"How serious is this?" Chloe asked.

"How long has this been going on?"

"It's been getting pretty serious. He wants me to meet his mom."

"Oh!" Jewel put her hand on her hip.

"It started at the end of August, when I started the program, and I really, really like him."

"Okay, then. Have all the fun your mind and body can handle," Jewel said, raising her glass.

"Look at you, glowing and blushing," Chloe teased.

Jade shared everything, including the fact that their dad had warned her to stay away.

Jewel's and Chloe's eyes widened at that bit of information. They knew how hard it could be to gain the approval of their parents when it came to significant others, especially El. But this time it was Bobby Dale who already didn't approve. Jade had to find a way to deal with that.

"Listen. If he's the one that makes your heart sing happy little love songs, then Dad will have to come around. If Mom could come to accept Donovan and Sterling, you'll be just fine." Jewel brushed off Jade's anxiety.

"Oh, she definitely won't approve. He didn't come from a perfect pedigree. In fact, he hails from very, very modest means and was raised by a single mom."

Simultaneously, Jewel and Chloe gasped, holding their hands over their hearts before cracking up laughing.

"How did all three of us manage to defy poor El's wishes of bringing home perfectly pedigreed knights in shining armor?" Jewel said. "I just knew she was going to faint when she found out about Sterling being divorced and having a kid."

"Yeah," Chloe said. "You broke the mold with that one!"

"And I would do it all over again," Jewel said proudly, pouting her lips.

"You'd better!" Jade added. "Both Sterling and my new little niece are the bomb!"

All three laughed and continued to share stories and drink wine. Jade adored her sisters, and despite being nervous about sharing Nixon with them, she felt free after their talk. She'd handle her parents. Having her sisters' approval meant the world. This relationship between her and Nixon had moved faster than any other she'd been in, but he was everything she realized she wanted in a man—ambitious, funny, intelligent, considerate, handsome and incredible in bed. He didn't seem to be the least bit fazed about her being a Chandler. Most of all, he adored his mother and that was always an admirable trait in a man.

Jade had made her decision. After meeting his mother, she was going to introduce him to her family. Thanksgiving was coming up. That would be the perfect time. Jade's next thought made her mouth the word *"Wow."* Nixon's presence in her life had made her forget all about Mitch. If she wasn't sure whether or not she was over him before, she knew she was now.

Chapter 22

Nixon wasn't the superstitious type, yet was convinced that Jade had put a spell on him. She invaded every one of his senses, dominated his thoughts and made him crave her all the time. He loved the lingering of her scent. Her sweet voice was music to his ears. He could get lost in her pretty brown eyes. Jade's body curved and swelled in all the right places. Whether she wore jeans, pajamas, business attire or nothing at all, sexiness exuded from her. Her gentlest touch aroused him.

Even more than her body, he loved Jade's mind. In their project sessions, she'd come up with some of the most brilliant ideas. Early in their coupling, he felt completely comfortable around her and found himself sharing things that would normally take months for him to feel content enough to bring up with other women.

Nixon even told his mother about her. She had only smiled.

"This one really has you smitten, huh?" she'd said.

He couldn't deny it.

Nixon planned a special getaway for the two of them during their trip to California for the leadership training's culmination. That program had been intense, taking a full workday out of each week since the end of August. It carved itself into his spare time for their team's project meetings, which often happened weeknights and a few Saturday afternoons. However, Nixon didn't regret it at all. He'd learned so much about leadership and even more about himself. Best of all, he'd met Jade—the woman with a magical touch that electrified him and spun his world like a top. He hadn't even felt this compelled by his ex-fiancée.

Speaking of her, Nixon occasionally wondered what had become of his ex. It was as if she'd fallen off the face of the earth. It was clear that they weren't meant to marry and it was a good thing that they'd realized that before it was too late. But he wished her well nonetheless. She was a good woman—just not for him, nor was he the best fit for her. He hoped that wherever she was, life was being kind to her.

Nixon pulled up to meet his mother. Gloria was thoroughly wrapped in a cashmere coat and large scarf—her weapon against the extremely cool air for early November. Both had taken the day off from work to handle business for the properties they owned, and to take a look at others. It was time to add to their portfolio. They started with breakfast at one of their favorite diners in New Rochelle.

"Your usual table, my dears?" the mature woman who had been working at the diner for as long as Nixon could remember asked.

"Yep. How are you doing, Olive?" his mother asked.

From the raspy voice, leathered tan skin and wrinkles creasing her lips, Nixon imagined Olive had a heck of a past and now spent most of her days sipping bourbon and chain-smoking. Still, her presence made the diner an extension of home.

Olive grabbed two menus, tilted her head toward their regular booth and started walking. Nixon gestured for his mom to walk in front of him.

"I'm fantabulous! Can't you tell?" Olive responded. She always slathered the sarcasm on thick. "I'm here, aren't I? Eh." She shrugged.

Laughter erupted from Gloria and Nixon.

"Any day that I wake up on this side of the soil is a good day. The day I wake up dead…" Olive shook her head vigorously. "Oh boy, that day will be a problem! Ha!" Her laugh matched her raspy voice.

"You're too much!" Gloria said through her chuckles. They loved her gritty humor.

"That's what the ex-husbands said." She slapped her knee and placed their menus on the table at their favorite corner booth. Light filtered in from the windows that met at a ninety-degree angle. "Have a seat and I'll bring your tea." She pointed to Gloria. "And your coffee," she said, peering at Nixon over her glasses. "Are we ordering anything different today?"

"No, ma'am."

"Okay. I'll go ahead and put your orders in." Olive pulled a pad from her apron and confirmed their selections as she jotted them down. "Be right back."

Gloria smiled at her son across the table and patted his hand.

"What?" he asked, noting her Cheshire grin.

"Tell me about this little lady you've been seeing. She has an interesting effect on you."

Nixon didn't bother denying his mother's claim. His feelings for Jade couldn't be hidden.

"I want you to meet her."

"Let's make that happen."

Over their breakfast of an egg-white omelet filled with veggies for his mother, and pancakes, bacon and eggs for him, he brought her up to speed on the latest with Jade.

"Sounds like she might be 'the one.'" Gloria curled her fingers into air quotes.

"I can see that." Nixon nodded in agreement. "Maybe. Just maybe."

"Wow!" Gloria reared back. "You can? Are you telling me you just might be ready for marriage—for real this time?"

Nixon grinned and shook his head, yet he couldn't deny that it was true. They enjoyed their meal and left to handle business. Finishing up in time for lunch, Nixon dropped his mom home and headed back toward Long Island. Once he hit the Long Island Expressway, he dialed Jade's cell number.

"Hey." She sounded out of breath.

"Hey yourself! Were you running or something?"

"Running myself ragged playing firefighter. I'm just missing a hose, pumper truck and a uniform."

"Crazy day, huh?"

"*Crazy* doesn't even begin to describe my day."

"Have you eaten?"

Jade didn't answer right away.

"You can't keep running on all four cylinders without fuel."

"I know. I'll grab something soon. I promise. But thanks for your concern. It makes me think you really like me," she joked.

"I kind of do like you—a lot. A whole lot! You need

a real break instead of shoving lunch down your throat at your desk while you put out fires."

"I know, but there's so much to do."

Nixon decided right then that he would drive straight to her office and surprise her with an impromptu lunch date. "And you're about to tell me you have to go so you can jump into the next fire."

"Sorry?"

"No apologies necessary. Talk to me for a while, let me be your break."

"Sounds like you're in the car. Coming from a meeting?"

"Yes. Are you going to let me be your break?"

Jade huffed. "Yes. I really do need one."

"Good. No talking about work."

Nixon kept her on the phone for the next twenty minutes, getting off only to stop at a florist and pick up a bouquet of roses to show up with at her job. He promised to call her back in a few minutes.

"Hey," she said, when she picked up the phone this time.

"Has the building burned down yet?"

"No, silly, but I'm glad you called. I have to admit it did calm me a little. Things have been so busy we haven't talked about work lately."

"Work is the last thing I want to spend time talking about when I'm with you. Especially on weeks like this."

"I know. I miss you. Can't wait until Friday."

Nixon glanced at his watch as if it told the passing of days instead of time in minutes and hours. "You mean I'm not going to see you until Friday?"

"I'm afraid not. I have several evening commitments this week."

"Then you really leave me with no choice."

"No choice for what?" Jade asked.

"I'll call you right back." He ended the call abruptly.

Nixon pulled up to the security booth at her building complex, gave his name and showed his ID. The guard let him pass. When he saw a man walking through the parking lot, he hurried into a spot and caught up with him by the time he reached the door since he didn't have a security pass. Nixon laid the dozen red roses aside while he signed in to the building at the front desk and then headed toward the foundation's offices.

Inside, he stepped carefully, listening for Jade's voice, which he heard talking about vendor contracts. A few people looked up at him carrying the beautiful bouquet and he put his fingers to his lips. They watched in smiling awe, waiting for the person the flowers were intended for to notice. Nixon continued toward her voice. Her office door was open. Nixon heard her and another voice that sounded interestingly familiar. He couldn't quite place it. He continued on through the office and tapped on her door, hiding behind the bouquet.

"I'm here with a special request to take the lovely Ms. Chandler out to a much-needed lunch."

Grinning, Nixon lowered the flowers to see the surprised look on his sweetheart's face. What he saw wiped his grin away. Jade's smile fell right after his and her expression registered confusion.

Alyssa stared at him in awe. "Nixon?"

"Alyssa?"

Jade's brows scrunched. "You two know each other?"

"Nixon was my fiancé."

Chapter 23

Jade stood frozen while the scene she'd just witnessed played in her head. Alyssa and Nixon. This couldn't be possible. *This isn't happening*. She blinked. Jade blinked again. Alyssa and Nixon were still standing in her office. The air was thick with awestruck tension.

"Nick, what are you doing here?"

Did Alyssa, her best friend from college that she was so elated to reconnect with, the one she'd hired to work for her, just call her boyfriend a nickname? The man she'd developed such strong feelings for was that same friend's former fiancé? Nick? Nixon?

The fact that Alyssa had called him something other than "Nixon" stung. In that simple word, the history they shared became tethered to the reality that stood in front of Jade. She didn't know whether to stand or sit. She chose to sit, not sure how much more her legs could bear under the weight of all this confusion.

Weren't there over ten million people in the New York metro area, including the surrounding suburbs? How had this happened? Jade had finally admitted to herself that Nixon was perfect for her. She'd gleefully told her sisters about him. They gave her the license and go-ahead to move forward. He wanted her to meet his mother. She was planning to have him meet her parents.

Slowly, the words that Alyssa and Nixon had been exchanging blossomed from the distance. She had seen their lips moving, but nothing registered.

"...for a few years now," Jade heard Nixon say. Sound finally registered right in the middle of his sentence.

"Oh, uh, well..." Alyssa cleared her throat. "And you two are dating?" Alyssa looked confused. Her stammering caught Jade's keen attention. The haze from moments before was now completely gone. She watched as Alyssa continued to speak. "Since when?"

Jade noticed Alyssa wince.

Somehow, Nixon was standing behind Jade, with his hand on the back of her shoulder. Jade didn't remember seeing him walk to her. Nixon handed her the flowers, leaned forward and kissed her forehead. She felt like she'd kissed her boyfriend in front of her father.

"We've been seeing each other for a while now. It's gotten pretty serious," he answered.

Alyssa's eyes narrowed. Jade looked at her and her friend's face softened.

"Oh. Well. I guess that's nice." Alyssa's eyes were back on Nixon's.

This was too much. Jade blinked and shook her head one more time.

"I hope things are good with you, Alyssa." Nixon's words were kind. Genuine.

"Oh yes. Of course. Pfft." She waved her hand. "Things

are great. I'm working here…with Jade now…as the program director. So far it's been amazing. How often do people get to work with their best friends? Yeah…things are great."

Jade looked from Alyssa to Nixon. It felt like she was in the middle of an emotional tug-of-war. Both of them seemed to be marking their territory.

Jade stood so abruptly she arrested the attention of both of them. "Alyssa, will you excuse us, please?"

At first, Alyssa just stared, as if she wasn't sure what Jade had said. Then she looked at Nixon—or Nick, as she would have said—and her eyes again narrowed ever so slightly.

After a while, she said, "Sure. I'll be in my office." And she turned on her heels and left.

Jade walked over and closed her office door. Folding her arms across her chest, she paced. What was she supposed to do? To whom did she owe loyalty?

"Jade."

She continued pacing.

"Jade!" Nixon's voice was sharp.

Jade stopped pacing and looked at him. "I…"

"Let's go to lunch. We'll make it quick."

Jade let her hands fall against her hips with a slap. She was still torn, but obliged. Grabbing her coat and purse, she headed through the office with Nixon holding her hand. She felt as if all eyes were on her as they exited. In her head, she heard their whispers. That talk had already begun. Jade never wanted to be the center of gossip.

Nixon took Jade to a local bistro. For the first twenty minutes or so, few words passed between them. The clanging of forks and knives against plates and the rumble of nearby voices were the only sounds for a while.

"What are you feeling?" he finally asked.

"Awkward. Torn." Jade stirred her spoon around in her soup, but didn't eat. Her salad was untouched, as well.

"Eat."

Jade sighed. "Who would have ever thought?"

"Yeah. Small world."

"You know the unwritten rule."

Nixon put his hand up. "What I do know is what we have now. Neither of our pasts should affect that."

Jade's shoulders deflated. Nixon was right. She still felt torn, but he was still right. They'd built something wonderful over the past few months. They craved each other. Enjoyed each other's company. Adored one another's intellect. The only thing that kept them apart was their busy work schedules. If too many days of work stood in the way, they'd sleep over at each other's house and go to work from there. It didn't matter if half a night of sweet lovemaking gave them delicious sex-hangovers the next day. Was she supposed to give that up? It wasn't like she knew he'd dated Alyssa before. They had lost touch—for years! Jade didn't steal Nixon from Alyssa. She'd never do such a thing.

"Jade."

"Huh?" She'd done it again—gotten so lost in her thoughts she hadn't heard him calling her name.

"I know this must be really weird, but what we have is *ours*. We built this. This is *our* connection. We don't owe anyone anything."

"I know."

They finished their meal mostly in silence. At least Nixon finished his. Jade had hers wrapped and took it back with her to the office. She was happy to have gotten out of the office when she did. The air had become too thick and she needed to breathe. Nixon insisted on walking her back inside, with his hand in hers the same way they'd walked out.

Jade could feel the stares from her staff—including and especially Alyssa's. Nixon walked her to her office, closed the door behind them and wrapped Jade in his arms. She exhaled and melted into his embrace. She stayed there. Being in his arms had become one of her favorite things.

Nixon lifted her chin and kissed her. "We're not doing anything wrong. I…" He paused.

Jade wondered what he was going to say. She felt like she knew.

"You need to get back to work. Call me on the way home." He kissed her one more time.

Nixon kissed her with more than just his lips. Jade felt his soul wrap around her like a blanket. It warmed her. It stirred her own soul. Nixon kissed her as if he had something to say that his words alone couldn't express. She thought he wasn't going to let go. She allowed herself to get lost in his kiss. Felt his passion and something else that felt like love. Jade felt weightless in his arms. And then there was a tiny explosion in her core. The blast sent a blaze of heat through her core. She held him tighter. Pulled him closer. Felt him rise against her and had to remind herself of all the people right outside her office door.

Just as she forced herself to remember her current location, Nixon ended the kiss with a few sweet pecks. He caught his breath.

"Come to me tonight."

Jade nodded, breathed deep and let it out slowly as she watched him walk out her office door and close it behind him. He must have known she needed a moment to gather herself. Before she could fully pull herself together and descend from the cloud that Nixon's kiss had left her on, there was a tap on her door.

She barely finished saying, "Come in," when Alyssa stepped in and shut the door.

Chapter 24

Jade hadn't come to him that night. Somehow he knew she wouldn't. Nixon wasn't going to press the issue. He wanted to give Jade the time she needed to sort this out, but not too much. The few days he'd already spent without consistently hearing her voice or responding to a barrage of humorous or sexy texts filled with innuendos already felt like too much time had passed. He didn't know what to expect at their upcoming weekly session or project meeting. He'd managed two days of simply worded greetings in the morning and late at night.

To settle his mind, Nixon threw himself into his work. And like the previous days, he had this one planned to the minute. Arrive early. Work on team project deliverables during lunch. Work late. Go to the gym. This schedule would give him little time to contemplate how much he'd miss Jade. She'd become such an integral part of his life that gaping craters had formed in her absence.

If he didn't have time to notice them, maybe he wouldn't feel so empty. What troubled him most was that while he wasn't able to reach her, Alyssa had full access to Jade during their workday.

Nixon still wondered how they'd missed that connection. He and Jade spoke about every era of their lives from childhood up to the moment they'd met. He'd known how close she was to her cousin Kendall and her sisters, but never once heard her mention Alyssa. Maybe she did, but he didn't make the connection that it could possibly have been *that* Alyssa.

Nixon reached for his keys and cell phone and headed to the door. The phone rumbled in his hand. He checked his alerts as he took it off Vibrate. The first notification was from his calendar. It was his father's birthday. Nixon stood still and inhaled. He blew that breath out and remained unmoving for several more moments. This would change his plans.

Nixon dialed his mother once he entered the parkway.

"How's my favorite lady?" He hoped that his mood hadn't seeped into his tone.

"Fine as wine. And how's my favorite son?"

"Mom. I'm your only son."

"Hee hee!" Her giggle brought a genuine smile to his face. He needed that. "On your way to work, babe?"

"Yep. You?"

"I'm already here. I'm on the early shift. Permanently."

"Really?"

"I know. Can you believe that? These days I like getting home earlier. Call it age, but at nine o'clock I'd much rather roll over in my bed than to be rolling on that bumpy highway."

"You're getting—"

"Watch it…!" She stretched her words, warning him.

"Finer. I was going to say *finer*, as in wine." Nixon laughed.

"You better had." After her chuckle she asked, "What are you doing later?"

Nixon knew where this was going. "How come you still do this?"

"Because I'm not mad at him. I let that go a long time ago." Nixon huffed at her answer. "I know your father. I understand him."

"But he abandoned us, betrayed us."

"He had his reasons."

"How can you say that?"

"Sweetheart. You can't expect more from people than they expect from themselves. I learned that a long time ago, too. Besides, he's not as bad as you think. He's just broken. He really does care about you. He just doesn't know how to show it."

"I don't believe that and I don't understand you when it comes to him."

"Nicky." Her tone was full of warmth. A lump grew in Nixon's throat at the sound of his mother's nickname for him. "I spent years being mad at your father. I blamed him for tearing our family apart until one day I realized that he hadn't taken anything from me that I needed in my life. I had you. I also realized that his leaving released me from trying to bear the weight of his brokenness. The whole time we were married, I tried to fix him, when I should have moved aside to let him fix himself. At some point he realized the same thing, and that's when we finally got to a point where we could have a decent conversation and eventually became something akin to being friends. I accepted what we'd become and so did he."

"So that kept him from being a father?" Nixon's voice

shook. His throat locked. He had to clear it several times before he could speak again.

"What else?" his mother asked calmly.

"What do you mean, what else?"

"What else do you want to say, son? What's hurting you?"

Nixon's pride wanted to say that nothing hurt. That he was a grown man—a successful one at that. That he'd gotten to where he was without his father and didn't need him anyway. Instead of answering, he blinked. His eyes stung. He blinked again. His lips tightened until his teeth were clamped shut. His jaw was set so tight he began to feel the pressure in his temples.

The truth was he had a lot to say. For years he'd kept it all in. The boy in him had things to say. The unruly teenager had things to say and the man who was forced to ride the rough waves into manhood unguided had even more to say. Nixon was afraid if he started he might never stop. In the end what difference would it make? He and his father would never become "something akin to friends."

How could his mother be so accepting? Nixon almost felt betrayed by her cavalier perspective. Hadn't he abandoned both of them? Hadn't he left her to struggle to raise a young black man all by herself?

Where would forgiving his father get him now? He'd tried that before. He'd done things for his father that his father had never done for him as a child. The home his father lived in was owned by Nixon and his mother. What difference would it make? Would it finally get his father to see him? To really see him? To care? To for once act like he was proud of all he'd accomplished, despite not having help from him? To love him?

"Tell me what else, son."

"What do you want me to say?"

"I just want you to let it out. You've held on to this for years. You need your release."

Nixon gripped the steering wheel. His knuckles changed hues. His chest heaved. Eyes stung. Nixon wanted to, but refused to make a sound. He couldn't. If Nixon opened his mouth, he didn't know what would come out.

His mother waited on him. Finally, she said, "Will I see you tonight? Please come. For me, sweetie. I love you." His mother ended the call.

Nixon blinked again and a tear rolled down his cheek.

Chapter 25

Jade looked at the time illuminated on her dashboard. Normally she would be in conversation with Nixon as they rode to work. She wondered who he might be speaking to instead. She thought to call him but changed her mind. She'd send him a text when she got to work. She wasn't ready to hear his voice.

Distancing herself from Nixon tore her apart. Reminders of him lived everywhere. His sneakers were in her front closet. His favorite toothpaste inside her vanity mirror. She could feel phantom caresses in that odd place between being awake and asleep. He'd meet her in her dreams, where everything was back to normal. The greatest impact was due to the hole in her heart. She thought back to the other day in her office. Nixon was about to say that he loved her. Jade could feel it. At first she wondered if she loved him, too. But now she wondered what that could mean in the midst of the situation that found itself at her feet.

Alyssa had come into her office when she got back from lunch to warn her about all the things she felt Jade needed to know about Nixon. He was sure to break her heart, she'd said. Alyssa also said that Nixon wasn't capable of committing. He'd probably bail on her when things got too serious. Who was Jade to believe?

The next day Alyssa had asked if Jade planned to fire her, because she desperately needed her job. Despite the awkward atmosphere that had taken up air in the office, Jade hadn't considered firing Alyssa. She felt bad that Alyssa had even asked. What had her friend thought about her?

Jade confided in Kendall, who told her to keep a keen eye on both Alyssa and Nixon and to take her time coming to a conclusion.

"Let them do all the talking," her cousin advised. "If something shady is going down, it will come up."

Jewel told her that the unwritten "no dating friends' boyfriends" rule didn't apply in this situation. "It's not like you guys were hanging out when she was engaged to him. Why should your happiness be compromised?"

Chloe just told her to follow her heart.

None of their advice helped. Alyssa was a good friend to Jade. She'd enjoyed getting reacquainted, swapping old, funny college stories and going out for drinks after long days at work. Alyssa was doing an amazing job running the foundation's programming department and had even been instrumental in helping prepare for the annual charity ball.

It was obvious that Jade dating Nixon made Alyssa uncomfortable and she'd known Alyssa so much longer. She could only imagine if the shoe were on the other foot. But Nixon had captured her heart—fitted himself snugly into the seams of her existence. She felt safe and content in his arms. The circumstances had Jade constantly grappling with her feelings. She didn't know how she was going to respond to seeing him in their session the next day. She'd been avoiding him to get her head right. She wouldn't be able to avoid him at the program.

Jade was surprised to find Alyssa in the office when she arrived. She'd intended to have time alone before the staff started to arrive.

"Hey," Alyssa said, as Jade walked past her door.

"Oh. Hey. Didn't expect to see you here so early."

"Yeah." The two stood still as seconds ticked away. "Can we talk?"

"Sure. Come to my office."

Jade truly didn't want to deal with this so early in the morning, but having these conversations while staff was in the office wasn't an option.

Jade tossed her coat across the back of her chair, sat and powered on her computer.

"I need some caffeine. Want a cup?" Jade preferred a glass of wine, but she was at work and hadn't even hit nine o'clock in the morning, so the coffee would have to do.

"Good idea." Alyssa accompanied Jade to the kitchen and filled her cup with milk and sugar while Jade took hers with a touch of vanilla-flavored cream.

"Okay." Jade put her cup down on her desk and sat back.

Alyssa grunted before she began to speak. "This is so uncomfortable. I know I spit out some crazy things the other day after seeing Nixon. But now I want to tell you what happened between us and why I said those things."

"Um-hmm." Jade sipped the steaming liquid, bracing herself for both the heat against her lips and what Alyssa had to say.

"He practically left me standing at the altar."

Jade sat up straight. "What?"

"Well. Not the day of the wedding." Alyssa sighed. "He walked out of my life two weeks before." Alyssa was sitting and stood. "It was so embarrassing. It was supposed to be a small ceremony but we had family coming from all over. Travel plans had been made. The reception hall was paid for and everything." Alyssa threw her arms in the air. "I couldn't believe it." She was pacing now. "He came to my apartment to talk. Told me he couldn't do this anymore. We were having issues, but it wasn't anything we couldn't work out. I made dinner. Left my engagement ring on the microwave while I prepared the meal. We started arguing. I told him to leave. After he left, I realized the ring was gone." Alyssa stopped moving and folded her arms across her body, hugging herself. She stared off into nothing. Stayed that way for seconds that felt like minutes. "Just like that, my engagement was over."

Jade thought Alyssa would cry, but didn't see tears fall. Jade went to her side and rubbed her back. Here she was, comforting the woman who used to date her boyfriend because he'd left her.

"He'll charm you." The words rushed from Alyssa, startling Jade. She looked at Jade with wild eyes. "He'll make you think he loves you. Have you feeling like you're the only person in the world that matters, and when things get too serious, he's out the door. He'll break your heart, Jade!" she pleaded. "One woman isn't good enough for him. It never was. He was Nick the player. You see how good-looking he is. Women can't take their eyes off him. I was always competing. He can't be loyal. It isn't in him." Alyssa finally sat down in the chair across from Jade's desk. She seemed spent. Her chest heaved up and down.

Jade wasn't sure what to say. "I'm so sorry that happened to you."

"That's why I stayed away the last time. From what I heard, he quickly moved on. I'd hardly gotten settled in my next location and he was on to the next woman. I hadn't seen him again after that day…until Monday."

Jade reared her head back. "Before Monday, you hadn't seen him since the day he broke off the engagement?"

Alyssa offered a solemn shake of her head. Jade now understood why her anger seemed so fresh.

Jade sat down. "Wow!" Jade wasn't sure if this made things better or worse. "How long has it been?"

"Two years."

Chapter 26

Despite his reluctance, Nixon was on his way to meet his mother and father for dinner. Even as he crossed the Throgs Neck Bridge, he wondered if Nick Sr. would actually show up, and wished it didn't matter so much.

The conversation with his mother on his way to work earlier nagged at him all day. He had carried that angst through the workday, over lunch, and now he dragged it along the New England Thruway. Gloria was right; Nixon had never truly expressed his feelings about his father to anyone, not even to her. Families with resources sent their kids to therapy to deal with their feelings. Gloria couldn't afford that, so Nixon kept them bottled up, preferring to pretend it hadn't affected him. His accomplishments were supposed to support this claim. Instead he secretly waited for his father to tell him that he was proud of him at least once. Yet it didn't seem to matter that the son of a struggling mechanic had risen out of the ashes of a broken existence like a phoenix. His father refused to acknowledge how he'd managed to make a comfortable life for him and his mother, where they would never have to worry about struggling again. Nixon had worked several jobs during and after college and had become an astute, successful businessman. That mattered. Didn't it?

Just because his mother hadn't raised a total jerk, Nixon got his father a birthday card and slipped a five-hundred-dollar Visa gift card inside. No matter what, he knew his father could use the money. If he didn't show up, Nixon would give it to his mother.

Nixon got to the restaurant early enough to watch both his father and mother arrive. His father was still driving an old Chevy that he'd repaired and polished for years. Nixon couldn't remember if Nick Sr. had ever owned a late-model vehicle, let alone a luxury car.

Nixon took several cleansing breaths before turning off the car and making his way into the restaurant. Like their old favorite diner, Nixon and his mother were familiar with this trendy establishment. Mount Vernon and New Rochelle were both small towns that bordered each other. New Rochelle boasted a more affluent existence in some parts and was home to famous residents like Ossie Davis and Ruby Dee. Nixon had grown up in Mount Vernon and aspired to a life in New Rochelle before turning that in for Long Island, to take his current position.

The owner of the restaurant was a local artist and musician that his mother had known for years. His own art decorated the walls of what had become a local hot spot. Their award-winning cuisine kept people flowing through the doors on a daily basis. This wasn't the kind of place that his father frequented, except when he accompanied Gloria.

"Hey, Nixon!" Chase, the owner's son, greeted him

with a masculine hug and pat on the back. "It's been a long time. How you doing, man?"

"Pretty good. I can't complain. How about you?"

"Life has been good. Your parents are over there." Chase pointed.

"Thanks, man. It's good to see you." Nixon made his way to the table Chase gestured toward.

"Hey, honey." Gloria rose to hug him.

"Hey," his father said.

"Hello," Nixon said back. He stood for a clumsy moment before pulling out his chair to sit.

Gloria smiled. Normally, his mother's beautiful smile penetrated his mood, regardless of what he was feeling. This time that didn't happen.

"It's nice to be out with the two of you together." She patted both their hands and picked up a menu. "What are we having today, Nicky?"

Gloria was trying, but the brick that seemed to settle in his chest wouldn't allow her warm words to change his cool demeanor. Nixon picked up his menu and opened it. He felt his father watching him but didn't look up.

"Oh. Happy birthday," he said after a while and placed the card on the table.

"Thanks." His father's replies were just as short. He picked up the menu, leaving the card in the spot where Nixon had left it.

"Order whatever you want, Nick. It's our treat," Gloria said, browsing her own menu.

Nixon drew in a deep breath and let it out in a sharp exhalation. He couldn't remember a time when Nick Sr. treated them to anything.

"I appreciate it," Nick Sr. said. His tone was still guarded.

"Try the lamb chops. They're delicious. I'm sure you'll love them."

"Okay."

Their waiter came, poured Nixon wine, refilled his parents' glasses and took their orders. Nick Sr. and Gloria conversed around him. Nixon hadn't bothered seeking an entry into their conversation. Instead he stewed, becoming angrier by the minute. It seemed that all the years of silence were boiling toward this very moment. He was afraid to open his mouth. He and his mother's earlier conversation had opened a lid that refused to close. Hot words bubbled in his throat. He pushed them back down with hard swallows, trying to keep his emotions from erupting steaming lava all over their dinner.

"Open your card, Nick," Gloria said cheerfully.

That snagged Nixon's attention. Nick Sr. hesitated, but eventually reached over their plates to retrieve the envelope. He pursed his lips and held the card another moment before tearing it open.

"What does it say?" Gloria asked.

What did she expect it to say? He hadn't exactly been the father of the year. Nixon had carefully selected the card that said the least about fatherhood. It could very well have been given to a stranger and held more warmth. Nick Sr. opened the card and the Visa credit card fell out. He frowned. A frown? Nixon swallowed, pushing the heat on his tongue into his esophagus, hoping it didn't lead to heartburn. But hadn't his heart already burned enough?

"I'm sorry. I can't take this." Nick Sr. placed the card by Nixon's plate.

"Nick…!" Gloria stretched out his name. "Why? It's a nice gesture from your son."

"I…"

"Don't worry, Mom." Nixon held his hands up. "I'm used to his rejection."

"Nicky!" There was a warning in her tone. She touched Nixon's arm.

"No. Really. I don't even know why I bothered to come." The volcano began to erupt and Nixon couldn't stop it. Being aware of the other patrons, Nixon leaned closer to the table and spit in a high whisper, "You can't help yourself, can you? You always have to find a way to shoot me down. Does that make you feel better for being such a horrible dad?"

Nick Sr. reared back and blinked hard as if Nixon's words physically struck him in the face.

"Nicky!" Gloria called his name with more authority.

"With all due respect, Mom, you asked what I wanted to say. I'm going to say it now. All of it." Gloria's mouth opened slightly. Nick Sr. huffed. "And you're going to hear me out." Still whispering, Nixon looked around before continuing. "You walk out on us for years, leaving us to struggle and climb out of a hole you helped to create. I needed you. We needed you, but you didn't care." Nixon's sight blurred, but he kept speaking. "Do you know how many times I sat in that living room window waiting for you to come and you never did? Why? Even as an adult you fed me nothing but broken promises. You still barely show up. But I made it without you. Mom and I don't struggle anymore. I made it," Nixon repeated, poking his chest. "Even though you weren't there when I needed you the most. And until now, not once have you said 'Good job, son,' or 'I'm proud of you.' Not once!" Nixon hit the table and everyone jumped.

Spittle flew from Nixon's tight lips.

"Despite that, I've tried and tried to be a good son and

for what? For you to throw my efforts back in my face each and every time? What have I ever done to you?"

"Nicky, please." Gloria's words were gentler now. She rubbed Nixon's arm.

"Nothing," Nick Sr. said.

"What?" Gloria said. Her hand went to her heart.

"You didn't do anything, son. I saw how well you and your mama were doing without me and figured you didn't need me messing things up. I always made things worse. That's why I don't take anything from you. I don't deserve it." Nick Sr. blinked and tears fell from his eyes.

Gloria's hand now flew to her mouth and tears rolled down her cheeks.

Nixon's chest heaved. Suddenly the air was too thick and hot for him to breathe. As he tried to suck in enough air to prolong his life a few more moments, his father's words sounded in his mind. He thought about all the times his father had rejected his attempts at making amends in some way. *I don't deserve it.* Had he just really said that?

"Who am I to speak of how proud you've made me when I haven't contributed to the man you've become?" Nick Sr.'s voice was surprisingly even. "I've always wanted to be a father to you. I didn't know how to insert myself back in. I still don't have anything to give. I'm sorry. I'm truly sorry." Nick Sr. stood. He gently placed his napkin on the table. "Thank you for tonight." He opened his worn wallet, pulled out twenty dollars and laid it on the table, as well. Then he left, leaving Gloria in awe, Nixon to catch his breath and the gift card under the napkin.

Chapter 27

Jade was still reeling about what Alyssa had shared as she drove to the leadership session. She wasn't ready to see Nixon yet. How could she blame him for what went wrong with his and Alyssa's relationship two years before? It was clear that Alyssa was still affected by it, which added to Jade's discomfort.

Jade had heard Alyssa's side. Nixon deserved to be heard, as well. Besides, this couldn't continue to linger. It wasn't like things would get any easier. Jade held her breath as she walked into the conference room where their classes were being held. She didn't see Nixon. She exhaled. Realizing she'd left her binder in the car, she grabbed her car keys, put her bag down and ran for the door, smacking right into Nixon's chest as he entered. The impact knocked the wind out of her.

"Nixon! I'm sorry."

He held her by both arms to steady her. "Good morning."

"Good morning." Jade wanted to kiss him. She looked into his red, tired eyes and wondered what had happened. Had they been speaking, she would have known already. She felt horrible that she'd been so distant at a time when he might have really needed her.

The weariness in Nixon's eyes spoke of much more than lack of sleep. Everything she felt for him came rushing down on her at once. She'd missed his handsome face, his sexy smile and those strong arms. They stood locked in place for a few seconds.

"I just need to run to my car," she said, feeling as if he deserved an explanation. He did, but not for this.

"Okay." They walked an awkward circle around one another.

Jade retrieved her binder and hurried back. Nixon was unusually quiet. He normally avoided her, but mingled with everyone else in the sessions. Today he sat alone with a cup of tea while they waited for everyone to arrive. He said very little as the program facilitator spoke of the upcoming summit and reminded everyone of when they needed to arrive in Newport Beach, California. He said even less during the actual session.

Just as they broke for lunch, Jade turned to him. "Can we talk?"

Nixon smiled. Jade knew it took effort. "Let's go outside."

On the way to the courtyard, Nixon's phone rang. He looked at the display. "Nine one four?" He looked at Jade and she shrugged. She figured it was someone from his old neighborhood. Nixon's number started with the same area code.

He tapped the phone icon. "Hello." Nixon's brows furrowed. Jade headed across the courtyard, giving him space.

The call was brief and he soon joined her on the other side.

"That was Alyssa," he said, taking a seat on the bench next to her.

"Alyssa?" Jade felt her heart lower with a bang. Why was Alyssa calling Nixon? Jade dismissed the uneasy feeling that crept over her. She wanted to ask what the call was about but refrained.

"I didn't know she still had my number. Anyway, let's talk about us."

"Yes. Us." Jade groaned. "I think I handled this whole thing badly, but I just don't know the right way."

"I can imagine how uncomfortable this must be for you, but I have to be honest—I'm more concerned about us. I know Alyssa is your friend, but we have something special and I'm not willing to let it go just like that. Have you talked to Alyssa about us?"

Jade kind of shrugged.

"What does that mean?" Nixon asked.

"I did more listening than talking. She really doesn't know much about us."

"So she told you about the breakup." He nodded knowingly.

"Yes. And I must admit, it scared me a little. How do I know you won't…?" Jade let her words trail off. She didn't want to hear herself say it and he didn't deserve to be judged like that.

"Different person. Different time. Completely different scenario."

"I know. It's hard. I was so excited to see her again. It seems like no matter what I do, it's not fair to someone. I'm sorry."

"Can we talk over dinner? I've missed you."

Jade felt her heart swell in her chest. She'd missed him

terribly, too. How could she say no? Despite Alyssa's warning, she and Nixon had something special. She needed to hear him out and this wasn't the place.

"Sure."

"I'll pick you up at eight."

She pursed her lips and nodded. They returned to the conference room and the atmosphere between them seemed lighter. She was also curious about what caused those red-rimmed eyes of his. She'd find out about that later, as well.

On the way home, she thought about reaching out to Reese. Maybe her insight would help. Jade dialed her number.

"Hey, Jade! You're coming to the wedding, right?"

"Of course. It was so great seeing you. We can never lose touch again, okay?"

"Okay. So what's up?"

"I need your insight." Jade updated Reese about the situation.

"Wow! That's a tough one. And I remember meeting him once or twice. He was a cutie." Reese hummed. Jade imagined her tilting her head with a finger to her chin. "I think it's a little unfair for Alyssa to encourage you not to be with him, though. It's not like you betrayed her purposefully. You had no idea that they'd ever dated."

"More than dated. They were getting married."

"Yeah. But still."

"What if it were you?"

"Sure, it would be awkward at first, but I wouldn't be mad at you—especially if things are going really well for the two of you. Who am I to stand in the way of that? What if you and he had the potential to have the most amazing relationship? Should you give that up? Look, it's obvious that you value your friendship. And if she values

it the same, she should be able to understand. Just give her
a little time. She'll come around. The real question is, how
do you feel about him and are you willing to lose that?"

Jade didn't want to lose Nixon. "Thanks, Reese! That
was helpful." Jade stayed on the phone with Reese until
she pulled into her driveway. Now she really looked forward to seeing Nixon later.

Jade felt better than she had in days. Before getting
ready for Nixon, she talked to her parents for a while
and then updated her cousin Kendall on what was happening. She took a long shower and slipped into a black
sweater dress that set her curves on display. She paired
it with black high-heeled boots and squirted her favorite
fragrance. Excitement coursed through her. Things between Nixon and her were going to be back on track and
she planned to make up for the lost time.

Nixon arrived right on time, looking more scrumptious
than she'd ever remembered. She drank in his tall frame,
swathed in a well-fitting black suit. His eyes still seemed
a little dull, but he smiled and those pearly whites of his
illuminated her soul. He had a manner that exuded suave-
ness and power. That was why he turned heads everywhere they went. Jade felt inclined to forget about dinner
and go straight to her room to start making up to Nixon.
How could she almost let him slip through her fingers?

"You look stunning!" He spun her around.

"And you look rather delicious." She shimmied into
her coat with his help.

"Shall we?" Nixon extended his elbow toward her.
Jade slid her arm through.

As soon as they were seated at the restaurant and had
placed their orders, Nixon wasted no time jumping into
the subject.

"Unfortunately, our relationship," he started, referring

to him and Alyssa at the time, "was over before it was officially over. We tried several times to make it work, but couldn't seem to get there. We broke up, got back together just to break up and get back together all over again. She didn't trust me and I couldn't understand why. I don't believe I'd ever given her legitimate reason not to. At one point I think she was more enamored with getting married than she was about making sure our relationship could work. She wasn't a bad person, but I couldn't see going into a marriage on such a rickety foundation. I suggested we wait and she lost it and told me if I didn't want to marry her then, there was no need to wait."

Jade didn't comment. She just listened.

"She used to go through my wallet and call numbers from business cards, even if it had a man's name on it. She accused me of hitting on her cousin, who was going to be her maid of honor. There's probably more that I could have done better to convince her I was faithful, but eventually I got tired of being accused."

Nixon paused as if he were waiting for Jade to interject. She remained quiet.

"The breakup was hard." He paused, reflecting. "I even thought about trying again, but knew it wouldn't work. It just wasn't meant to be."

"That's it."

"Were you expecting more?"

Jade shrugged. "I don't know. So the last time you saw her was when the two of you broke up."

"No. We'd run into each other a few times after the breakup. We have a few mutual friends. I figured we should at least try to be cordial so gatherings wouldn't seem so uncomfortable. She said she wasn't interested in being friends with me. It's been over two years since I've seen her."

"Hmmm." Jade hummed.

Nixon's take had her thinking. He didn't seem as bitter as Alyssa had.

"Are we finished with that? I want to get back to us."

"Yes. I'm sorry for the way I acted this week."

"No apology needed." Nixon took her hand. He looked right into her eyes. "Being away from you for those few days made me realize how much I want to be with you." Jade became aware of her own heartbeat. "I want to take this all the way."

Jade widened her eyes. "You mean all the way, as in *all* the way?" she asked, as if saying it twice would deepen the meaning.

"All the way as in *all* the way," he teased.

Jade threw her head back and had the heartiest laugh she'd had in recent days. Now she just needed to figure out a way to tell Alyssa she wasn't giving up Nixon.

Chapter 28

Nixon stepped inside Starbucks and rubbed his hands together. The chill in the air was biting and Thanksgiving hadn't even come yet. The winter was going to be bad. Nixon blew warm air into his cold hands and rubbed them again. He stepped in farther and looked around the bustling coffee shop. He spotted Alyssa in the corner near the back window, wearing a black hat and shades. Nixon wondered if this was her attempt at being incognito. He headed in her direction.

"Alyssa." He called her name when he approached.

She looked up suddenly, as if he'd startled her. "Hey, Nick. Have a seat." She removed her shades and smiled.

Nixon noticed she had a cup of something already, but asked if she wanted anything else. He ordered a cup of dark roast black and returned to the table where Alyssa sat.

Nixon wasn't in the mood for small talk. "I hope you're well."

"Yes. I am. Thanks. And you?"

"Great! What did you want to talk about?"

Alyssa sucked in a deep breath. "You look good."

"Thanks," Nixon said. "You called me. What would you like to talk about?" He put a lot of effort into being cordial.

"I needed to see where your head was."

"Why?"

"Do you really care about Jade?"

Nixon huffed. "Yes, I do."

"Do you love her?"

Nixon huffed again. He did love Jade, but hadn't told her yet. It wouldn't be fair if he'd revealed that information to Alyssa first. He didn't owe Alyssa any explanations. That time had passed.

Alyssa studied him, as if looking intently would glean an answer from him. "You love her," she determined. "Then why did you agree to meet me here?"

"Because you asked me to, Alyssa. What is this about?" She was starting to prick at his patience. Nixon had a long day ahead of him and wanted to get this part over with. He needed to know what was so important that Alyssa had to meet him early on a Saturday morning, anyway.

"I just needed to know."

"To satisfy your curiosity?" he asked.

"To know." Alyssa grunted. Nixon knew his response or lack thereof answered many things. "It's hard to see you with her." Alyssa focused on her cup, turning it in her hand. "We had something…special." She tucked her lips inward and then registered an awkward grin. "I needed to know if there was anything left."

Nixon took in a deep breath. "I can imagine how uncomfortable this must be for both of you."

Alyssa turned to the window. Nixon hadn't noticed

that she was crying until she reached up to wipe the tears slowly rolling down her cheek. After another moment she turned back to him, cast her eyes toward the table and spoke just above a whisper. "Maybe we could explore that. Fan the flames and see if they ignite."

"It's too late, Alyssa. Jade and I—"

Alyssa slapped the table. "I don't want to hear about Jade. I'm talking about us."

Nixon closed his eyes and took a breath. "Alyssa." He spoke in an exact manner, as if he were addressing a child. "There is no *us*. There won't be an us."

"There could be," Alyssa whined. Her tone was desperate, no longer irritated.

"I have to go, but I wish you well." As a parting gesture, Nixon placed his hand over hers. Alyssa looked at his hand and then snatched hers away.

"Fine. You'll just break her heart like you did mine. Don't come running after me then. That family is all about pedigree and you two don't have the same pedigree. You'll never be good enough."

Nixon stood, bade her a good day and left. He wished her well. Wanted her to find happiness even if it wasn't with him. Somewhere out there was a man who would adore Alyssa's erratic manner. Nixon hoped he'd come along soon.

On the drive over to Jade's, he had to work on his mood. Alyssa had ruined it. He had awakened excited about taking Jade to meet his mother.

Nixon picked Jade up and headed straight to Westchester. Mount Vernon and New Rochelle were his stomping grounds. He'd grown up there, became a man and went from pauper to prince within those town limits. Taking Jade around was like letting her see him on the inside.

Nixon started his tour in Mount Vernon, taking her to

the main streets where he and his friends had hung out. They passed by his high school and he told her about the day he'd cut school, but his mother found out and showed up at his friend's house where they were playing hooky.

"She should have been a detective, or signed up for the FBI or CIA. She had some crazy kind of sixth sense that would activate whenever I was doing something I had no business doing."

"I'm glad El wasn't that keen when I was a teen."

"I guess as an only child, I was all she had to focus on. It was like a game. I'd try to see how much I could get away with before she'd catch on. She always did. My friends' parents were oblivious."

"My parents cut their parenting teeth on Jewel and my brother, Chris. Chloe was by the book, so by the time I came along I could only get away with so much."

Nixon pulled over next to a small park. "Come on," he said to Jade. Nixon rounded the car, opened her door and held his hand out. Jade took it and leveraged her rise from the passenger seat. Hand in hand they walked into the park, while strong winds whistled around their ears.

Nixon led Jade to a tree and stopped. "It was under this tree that I had my first kiss." Jade chuckled and shook her head "Wait until you hear the rest. Her name was Katie Anderson. I had a crush on her since she came to our school in second grade. She was the only girl in sixth grade that had boobs and the boys gawked at her in giddy awe. It was like we couldn't understand how she looked like our parents and we were all in the same grade. The whole neighborhood hung out in this park. I heard a rumor that Katie liked me. My friends bet that she wouldn't let me kiss her. She was mean as hell, by the way. I told them getting a kiss from her wouldn't be a problem, since she liked me anyway. I brought her over to this tree. We talked for a few minutes. I asked if she liked me. She said, 'Maybe.' I went in for the kiss and she smacked the sight right out of me! I swear I saw into the next universe."

Jade burst out laughing. Nixon laughed, too.

"It was so embarrassing. In front of me, Katie stood glaring with her hands on her hips, and behind me was a chorus of my friends' laughter. I didn't live that down until high school. Every now and then, I'll run into Katie and we'll still laugh about it. She's married to a diplomat now."

"So your memories of this tree weren't so good, huh?"

"Nope!"

Jade leaned her back against the tree and tugged him toward her by his coat. "We can change that."

Nixon smiled, leaned forward and covered her mouth with his. Their kiss was passionate—a warm defense against the cold that left them hot and panting.

"Thank you." Nixon smiled and planted a few more pecks on her kiss-swollen lips, before taking her by the hand. "This tour isn't over."

"Take that, Katie!" Jade said, as they jogged back to the car. They were still laughing when they got back inside the warm vehicle.

Nixon drove past his childhood home and a few he currently owned with his mother. They headed into New Rochelle and took her past the homes of famous residents before finally arriving at the restaurant.

Nixon's mother was already inside chatting with the owner by the time he got there. When he walked in holding Jade's hand, a grin slowly spread across Gloria's face. She looked past him and settled her sight on Jade. Nixon thought he saw a small nod. He already had his mother's approval.

"Hey, Ma." He kissed her cheek.

"Hey, honey!" She squeezed him in her embrace.

"Jade, this is my mother, Gloria Gaines."

Jade held out her hand. "It's a pleasure to make your acquaintance, Mrs. Gaines." Jade channeled her proper mother, remembering her manners.

Gloria pushed her hand aside. Jade's eyes stretched wide. Gloria stepped in and wrapped her arms around her. "Mmm," she moaned, as she gave Jade a tight squeeze. "Any woman that has my son's heart doesn't get a handshake from me."

Jade laughed and wrapped her arms around Gloria, returning the sentiment.

Gloria pulled back. Holding Jade by her arms, she looked her over. "And you're beautiful. Come on." Gloria took her by the hand. "Let's talk." She led Jade away, leaving Nixon to catch up behind her.

Nixon jogged past them to pull out their chairs at the table. The waiter took their drink orders.

"Nicky tells me you run a foundation."

Jade glanced over at Nixon when his mother said his nickname, and suppressed a smile. Nixon tossed back a warning look but knew he'd get teased later anyhow.

"Yes, ma'am. We support organizations that empower children and college students in the areas of art, college and career readiness and leadership. We also offer grants to young entrepreneurs. That's really important to my parents—especially Dad."

"That's wonderful. I serve on the board of an organization here that offers scholarship help to students from high-need areas across Westchester. So do you want to tell me more about you or would you rather hear embarrassing stories about Nicky from when he was young?" Gloria winked at Nixon. He shook his head.

For the second time in the few minutes that she was in Gloria's presence, Jade's eyes stretched wide. She covered her laugh. Nixon tried to hold in his own laugh.

"Ma!"

"I'll take embarrassing stories about Nicky for one hundred, Alex," Jade teased, using the famous line from the game show *Jeopardy!*

Gloria threw her head back and cackled. One hand flew to her chest. "Oh, Nicky! Whew! I really like her."

The next two hours flew by as if they were minutes. Conversation and laughter came easy. Not only did Gloria share one or two embarrassing stories as she offered, she made her admiration for her son obvious by the way she doted on him and spoke so highly of all the wonderful things he'd achieved. Nixon's chest puffed as the two women spoke about how smart they believed he was.

It was something to watch his two favorite women engage and laugh even if he was, at times, the butt of their jokes. He didn't mind at all. That Gloria liked Jade wasn't a surprise. Nixon had had a feeling they would get along well.

Alyssa and Gloria never hit it off that well. Not one to stand in love's way, Gloria had stayed tight-lipped during their engagement. She'd always said her rejection was likely to drive him closer to her, and if they weren't meant for one another Nixon would eventually come to see that for himself. Distraught, Nixon had headed straight to his mother's house the day he broke off the engagement. She was even a little bit surprised. Gloria had only hummed "um-hmm" here and there as he shared the news. Then she'd stood by her Nicky when he was met with the backlash of Alyssa's family for canceling so close to the wedding date and "costing them so much damn money." Gloria had offered to pay them back every dime and they shut up. Every last one of them. Nixon and Gloria hadn't heard from them since.

But now something told Nixon that asking for Jade's hand in marriage would more than please Gloria. And Gloria's approval more than pleased him.

Chapter 29

The entire weekend had passed and the smile that radiated in Jade's heart still illuminated her mood. She and Nixon had spent the rest of the weekend at her house. On Sunday, they joined her sisters and brother with their significant others for brunch. The only thing left to do was to introduce Nixon to her parents. She thought back to their dinner with Gloria the other night and chuckled. By the time they'd finished eating, Jade was as smitten with Gloria as she was with her son and imagined what it would be like to have her as a mother-in-law.

"Whoa!" Jade almost hit the brakes in the middle of the expressway. Where had that thought come from? She laughed aloud. "Slow yourself down, little woman. It's only been a few months. You guys haven't even said the *L* word yet. Marriage is a little far off for now." She remembered that time she'd thought he was about to say it.

Could she love him? Did she love him? Jade was pretty

sure that what she was feeling felt a lot like love. When they were together, she never wanted time to run out on them. When she wasn't with him, all she could think about was being with him again. Her favorite place had become the crook of his arm. When they made love, it was as if she'd elevated to a higher plane and consciousness. A simple brush from Nixon was enough of a touch to cause an avalanche of need to rise within her. He made her laugh with her entire soul and smile with her whole heart. This had never happened before. Not even with Mitch.

Alyssa crash-landed right into Jade's thoughts. That was the other thing that she needed to handle. Alyssa had been warning Jade to drop Nixon hard and fast and run, for her heart's sake. She appreciated her friend's concern. This was a peculiar situation, but just like Reese said, Alyssa would come around. Wouldn't she? Jade had hoped so, because she wasn't giving Nixon up. She would pull Alyssa aside and chat with her about the situation when she got to the office. It was a necessary conversation, but she dreaded having to go there. She cared about her friend—valued their relationship. However, her cousin and sisters were right—that shouldn't dictate her relationships. Jade wasn't a home wrecker. She deserved Nixon and their relationship deserved a good try.

Jade started going over the conversation with Alyssa in her head as she drove. Thankful for a morning full of meetings, she hadn't made it to the office yet, but knew that as soon as she got there, Alyssa would be waiting. Jade thought about inviting her to lunch so they could have their conversation in confidence. She wanted Alyssa to know that she appreciated her concern, but despite that, she had strong feelings for Nixon. Hopefully, she would understand. It might take Alyssa a little time to get used to Nixon and Jade being together. What was the worst that could happen?

Jade pulled past the security gate into her building's parking lot. After easing into her designated spot, she sat in the car for several moments. Again, she went over the conversation in her head. Jade's fear was that Alyssa could still hold a flame in her heart for Nixon, which would make the situation worse. She tried to put herself in Alyssa's shoes and think about how she would feel, even though she believed her response would have been quite different. The last thing she wanted to do was hurt her friend's feelings. But this was Alyssa. She had always been a little possessive. Even as roommates in college, as close as they were, Alyssa was particular about how they divided their space in the room. Jade attributed that to her being an only child. With siblings, sharing had never been an option for Jade. It came naturally. For Alyssa, what was hers was hers and no one else could touch it.

Jade blew out a breath, opened the car door and stuck out one leg. She stayed like that for another moment before fully exiting the car. "Let's do this," she said, standing to her full height. She lifted her chin, squared her shoulders and made her posture erect enough to be mistaken for a ballerina. Jade waltzed into the building, down the corridor and into her office.

It was lunchtime and most of her small staff wasn't around. They were so dedicated they'd work through the entire day without stopping, so to restore balance, even in the midst of a high season, she mandated lunch be taken during certain hours to avoid burnout. She even tried to stick to the new rule herself, though she often failed.

As she passed Alyssa's office, she noticed the door was cracked. Jade looked around again. Everyone was gone. Her timing was perfect. She could have the conversation with Alyssa now while no one was there. Jade went to tap on Alyssa's door and heard something that caught her attention. Her hand was suspended just inches away. Instead of knocking, she inclined her ear toward the crack. Alyssa wasn't bothering to be quiet or discreet. The empty office gave her liberty. From the way her voice moved about, Jade could tell that she was pacing.

"Maybe she'll listen and stay away from him," Alyssa said to the person she was speaking to.

Jade assumed the "she" Alyssa was talking about was her and the "him" was Nixon. To confirm, she continued listening.

"I told her he would cheat on her—break her heart for sure." There was a pause. "I tried…" she continued, obviously still unaware of Jade's presence on the other side of the cracked door. "He made it clear that he wasn't interested in me anymore. That bastard…I think he actually loves her…Don't. Judge. Me!" she snapped at the person she was speaking to. "I had to do something. I can't stand the idea of him falling in love with her. Jade already has everything. She gets to have the one man I ever loved, too. It's not fair."

Jade pushed the door open and stood in the frame. Alyssa's head whipped around. Her mouth dropped and eyes bulged, but she quickly recovered.

"Yeah. Sure." She tightened her tone as if she could have been on a professional call. "Can I call you later? I have to go. Great. Thanks!" Alyssa ended the call and rubbed her hands along her thighs. "Hey, Jade."

Jade didn't bother returning a greeting. Instead, she pressed her lips together and narrowed her eyes at Alyssa.

"That w-was a friend," Alyssa stammered.

Jade tilted her head, continuing her glare. "Was it?"

Alyssa closed her eyes and huffed. "Listen." She sounded like she was ready to concede.

"I'm listening." Jade closed the space between them with slow, calculated steps.

Alyssa moved back, bumping into her desk. She rounded the mahogany wood structure, turning it into a barrier.

"It's not what it sounded like."

"Oh, really." Jade tilted her head more. "To me—" Jade poked her own chest. Anger sharpened her tone. "—it sounded like you tried to get in the way of me and the man I love." The word *love* slipped out. Jade noticed as it left her lips. Felt it on her tongue. Accepted it.

"You don't understand." Alyssa held her hands up.

"Oh. I understand perfectly. Why should I get to have Nixon, since I get to have everything else? Here I was concerned about your feelings because I thought you were my *friend*. You intentionally tried to destroy what I had with Nixon because you couldn't stand to see us together? How dare you?"

Alyssa's expression changed from one unrecognizable look to another and landed on irritation.

"How dare I? Oh, here you go. The spoiled little princess has to get every single thing she wants? Still?" Alyssa spit. Jade's mouth dropped. "Out of the millions of men in the New York metro area, you had to set your sights on *my* ex-fiancé. Come on! That's not the least bit suspicious. Apparently Jade still gets or *takes* whatever Jade wants."

"I didn't *take* anything from you, Alyssa!"

Alyssa sighed, dropped her head and her shoulders. "I'm sorry, Jade. Let's…let's just start over."

"That won't be necessary." Jade stood erect. "Thank you for your service here at the Chandler Foundation."

Her tone was professional. Direct. "You have fifteen minutes to be out of this building!"

Jade swiveled on her heels and left Alyssa right where she stood. Outside Alyssa's door, she met the wide, startled eyes of her staff, who'd just returned from lunch. "Get Security over here," she barked, then marched to her office and shut the door.

When she looked down, her hands trembled and hot tears stung her eyes. Jade swatted at them as if she were angry they'd even shown up.

Chapter 30

The energy at the leadership summit was exhilarating. During the opening night reception, Nixon met leadership fellows from programs across the country. Exchanging contact information with many of the attendees expanded his network exponentially. Executive leadership from the nation's top corporations led workshops and mingled with everyone. And the keynote speaker, a world-renowned professional life coach, had gotten everyone at the summit excited about their futures.

Nixon and his group were nervous about delivering their presentation before a panel of c-suite judges. Their team presented a business plan, explaining the product they'd designed using innovative technology to fill a need. Their presentation gained recognition as one of the top three, making them instantly famous for the remainder of the summit. The three-day event ended Saturday evening with a gala where each fellow from the program was awarded a certificate in executive leadership backed by one of the country's top business schools. A few alums of the program were also honored for notable accomplishments in their respective fields.

To keep their relationship low-key, Nixon and Jade booked separate rooms, even though Nixon slipped into Jade's and slept there each night. He'd rise early and return to his room, get dressed and leave from there. Their little game was still exciting to them even though they were sure several people in their cohort knew what was really going on—including Julia. She'd refrained from hitting on Nixon and had even become friendly toward Jade.

Early Sunday, mostly all the summit attendees were heading back home. Nixon and Jade took a short helicopter ride over to Catalina Island, where they rented a house for the night. Unlike back home, the skies were clear and the weather warm, with breathtaking views of the Pacific Ocean.

Nixon noticed Jade look at her watch several times as they strolled along the beach, and wondered why. Their flight wasn't scheduled to leave until the next morning, and as far as he knew, they purposely hadn't made any plans. This was a day for them to relax, since tight schedules awaited both of them when they returned to work.

Nixon stopped walking and pulled Jade into his arms. With her back to his chest, he pointed at the sea. "Look at that." He kissed her shoulder.

"Isn't it beautiful?" she said.

"Yep. That's what we should be focused on. We have all week to worry about the time."

Jade giggled. "Speaking of time!"

"What?" Nixon was confused.

"Look." Jade pointed down the beach.

Nixon followed her finger. Two men approached, guiding horses.

"Wha—"

"We're going to go horseback riding!" Jade squealed. "You said you've never been, right?"

"When did you do this?" Nixon thought they'd spent almost every moment together. How had she managed to set this up without him knowing?

"I set it up from home. Ready?" Jade bounced on her toes.

"Let's do this!" Nixon clapped and rubbed his hands together.

"Woo!" Jade ran off toward the horses, dragging Nixon behind her.

She slowed down as they got closer. Nixon assumed it was so they wouldn't startle the horses. He had to admit he was excited and glad to share this experience with Jade.

Nixon greeted the gentlemen walking the horses toward them. They signed a release and, after some brief instructions, mounted the horses, which gingerly carried them along the water's edge. Nixon hadn't anticipated how peaceful the ride would be. As the steeds clomped along the shoreline, Nixon closed his eyes momentarily and let the ocean breeze wash over him. He opened his eyes to see Jade's horse trotting in front of him. Her head was high and she had one hand out, letting the breeze flow through her hair and fingers.

Jade's sundress was hiked up to allow room to mount. She wore a bikini underneath, but the dress gave him an unrestricted view of the smooth skin of her thigh. Instantly Nixon's nature responded. He watched from behind as her bottom moved in time with the horse's gait, making him think about how in sync they moved together. After an hour, they returned the horses and found a restaurant with outdoor seating facing the water.

Nixon took in the environment as he sipped on a glass of merlot. A beautiful woman sat across from him. One who had arrested his senses from the first day he'd laid eyes on her. Gusts of air off the ocean lifted wisps of her hair. In the distance, turquoise water met an endless horizon. In another direction, beautiful beach homes held a cool majestic quality about them. The breeze carried a peace that didn't exist back home. Cherishing the moment, Nixon wished there was a way to bottle it and take it back with him.

As they sipped, words barely passed between them. Speaking wasn't necessary. They held hands across the table. Nixon set his eyes back on Jade. Admiring her beauty, he studied her and grinned. *Love.* The word floated across his mind as if it had been carried in the soft winds. Nixon had held back long enough. Long enough to allow doubt to dissipate—for confirmation to give him assurance. Long enough for it not to be too soon to say. Long enough to not care about the possible sting of rejection. What if she didn't love him back? It wouldn't matter. Nothing could change how he felt. He was sure of that. Nixon continued to examine her.

"What?" Jade asked, noticing him watching her.

"Nothing. Just taking in all this beautiful scenery, including you."

Jade's smile eased across her face. Her cheeks flushed.

"Are you blushing?"

"Maybe." She giggled.

Nixon lifted her hand to his lips and kissed the palm. "Let's go," he whispered. Desire made his voice husky.

Jade agreed with a seductive smirk. Nixon left money

for the wine and led her back down the beach to the house they'd rented.

Inside, they headed to the best part of the home. The back wall of the master bedroom was made of windows that showcased spectacular panoramic views of the ocean like a massive floor-to-ceiling painting. On the other side of the glass wall was a deck.

Nixon opened the wine fridge near the bedroom closet, poured two glasses of wine and met Jade out on the deck. He lay on the double chaise and patted the space beside him for Jade to occupy. She lay beside him with her head in the crook of his arm as they watched the sun set, casting flashes of orange, red and gold across the landscape.

"Thank you for today," Nixon said.

Jade turned to face him. "I'm glad you enjoyed it. I'm also glad we decided to stay an extra day. This is perfect." She looked toward the sky. He leaned over and picked up his cell phone so he could capture the image of her under the halo of the moon's soft light.

He wanted to say it right then, but wanted the time to be just right. Instead, Nixon kissed her lips. Her touch awakened his senses. He tasted her tongue. Ran his fingers through her hair. Nixon kissed her deeper than he ever had. His core responded first, tightening. An erection blossomed in his shorts. Jade's fingers roamed his taut chest, pushing his shirt up to feel his bare torso. A sliver of heat ignited in his loins and traveled to all the places she touched.

Nixon sat up. Jade stood, removed her sundress and bikini, letting the garments fall to her feet. Nixon followed suit, casting his shorts, boxers and T-shirt on the deck floor. She met his gaze. They spoke without words. Communicated unbridled need. She straddled him and flung her arms around his neck. His erection flinched, stood at attention, pressed against her center. Nixon stopped kissing her, forcing Jade to open her eyes and look at him. Her lips were still puckered. Gently, he took her face in his hands. She stared directly at him. He saw her need, felt her squirm against his manhood. She wanted him badly. He wanted her, too, but it was time.

Nixon lifted her slightly, sat her on him, slipping his elongated member inside her moist walls.

"Ahhh!" Jade's pitch rose. Her head rolled back. She convulsed a few delicious clenches against him.

Nixon pushed himself deeper inside. She rode him. They perfected their rhythm. Jade couldn't seem to keep her eyes open. She kept lifting her chin toward the sky as they moved in measured strokes against each other. Nixon's eyes threatened to roll back. He controlled his pleasure. He needed Jade to look at him. He needed to see her face. Once again he held her face in his hands.

"Jade." His voice was airy, as if it were blowing in the breeze. Her eyes were closed again. "Jade…" He panted. The pleasure she gave him was almost too much to bear. "Jade." His voice was slightly stronger. "Jade."

She looked at him. "Yes," she breathed.

"I love you." He drove himself deep inside her.

Jade blinked. Eyes wide now, she rode him. Blinked. Her chest rose and fell. "Nixon." Her voice was a sweet but anxious whisper.

"Yes." His response was husky.

"I love you, too."

Chapter 31

Jade was too anxious to sit still. This Thanksgiving was going to be the most memorable yet. She and Nixon were starting the day with his mother and then heading over to her parents' house for dinner with the Chandlers. When she returned from California, she'd called her parents to let them know she was bringing company for dinner. El interrogated Jade about where she'd met him, his background and why they hadn't heard about him before. The fact that Bobby Dale and El knew he was coming didn't keep the butterflies from circling her stomach like crows around a carcass.

Dinner at Mrs. Gaines's cozy home was tasty, fun but low-key compared to Chandler holiday gatherings. Gloria succeeded in making Jade feel right at home. They'd fallen into a natural rhythm of teaming up to tease Nixon. Gloria shared more stories that had Jade bent over laughing, but the mood changed when the bell rang.

Gloria opened the door and Nixon's father walked in, carrying a black plastic bag. Nixon was sitting at the dining room table and stood when his father entered the room. For several moments, they just stared at each other. Jade held her breath, but realized it only after several moments had passed. She held the edge of her seat. Gloria stood behind Nick with her hand over her heart. No one spoke. The tension choked the air out of the room.

Nick Sr. made the first move. He took one step closer to his son. Nixon stayed put. Jade wanted to touch his back—comfort him and let him know everything would be okay. She wanted to hold his hand and tell him to go ahead and talk to his father. She wanted to remind him how important it was to have him in his life even if he didn't think Nick Sr. was the best. She wanted them to get along, to begin to heal the pain she'd seen in Nixon's eyes whenever his name came up.

Nick Sr. took another step. Nixon still hadn't moved—hadn't taken his eyes off his father. Time slowed. Jade felt every heartbeat and stood suspended in the hope of what could happen. The four of them could wade in the tension, it was so thick. She willed Nixon's heart to soften. Inwardly, she rooted for whatever that was still broken in him to be mended.

Nick Sr. held out the black bag. "I bought you something."

Nixon reached for the bag. Gloria, Jade and Nick Sr. focused on that singular movement together, waiting for something to happen. Nixon took the bag and Jade exhaled.

"Thank you," Nixon said, standing tall.

"There's something inside beside the wine," Nick Sr. said.

Nixon opened the bag and pulled out a small card. He

looked up at Nick Sr., the question in his mind creasing his brow. Jade felt herself holding her breath again. Nick Sr. nodded, encouraging Nixon to open the card.

Nixon slid his finger across the opening of the envelope and pulled out the card. The front carried an image of a blue sky and a sun with gleaming rays that spanned the entire card. Script letters said *You Inspire Me*. Nixon flipped the card over, looked up at Nick Sr. again. Another nod—more silent encouragement. Nixon looked down, and for the next few moments, while time and breathing seemed to be suspended once again, he read the few handwritten lines. When he was done, Nixon swallowed hard. He cleared his throat, exhaled and looked toward the floor, blinking.

Jade wanted to know the words that made Nixon so silent.

"Well, what does it say?" Like Jade, Gloria was anxious.

"You can read it if you want to," Nick said.

Nixon cleared his throat once again. "'I've never been a man of many words, but you made me realize that I've left too much unsaid. I'm proud of you, son. I always have been. I can't help it. I admire the boy you used to be and the man that you've become. I hope we can find a way to start over. I hope you're okay with that. I'll understand if you don't want to. Either way, I needed to say this. And I hope you don't mind my putting these words on paper. Thanks. Love, your dad.'"

Gloria gasped. Tears flowed from her eyes. Jade's eyes watered. Nick Sr. shifted his weight from one foot to the other, turning his hat in his hands. He reminded Jade of a hopeful, wide-eyed little boy.

Nixon cleared his throat yet again. "I'd like that." He held his hand out toward his father.

Nick Sr. released the breath he'd been holding in a loaded exhalation. He pushed Nixon's hand aside and wrapped his arms around his son. It took a second, but Nixon soon hugged his father back. Gloria rushed over and swung her arms around both of them. Jade clasped her hands under her chin and let the tears that had gathered in the well of her eyes roll.

"Okay," Gloria said, pulling back. "What kind of wine is this, Nick?" She picked up the bottle and looked it over. "Whatever it is, it will be perfect for dessert."

"You made peach cobbler?" Nick asked.

"You know I did." Gloria twisted her lips. "It's Thanksgiving," she said, as if she needed to remind him.

Nick rubbed his hands together. "Great! I haven't had your peach cobbler in years."

The four of them gathered at the table. Gloria brought the pie out and set it in the center. Nixon handed dessert plates out to everyone.

"Wait!" Gloria held her hands up. "We need another grace." She bowed her head and thanked God for the food and mending the bond between father and son. "Now we can eat."

Conversation flowed lightly around the table, sprinkled with moans indicating how good the pie tasted.

"Nicky."

Nixon looked up at his father, pausing midchew. "You were probably wondering why I started coming around again. This is why. I was trying to figure a way to get back in with you. Thank you for giving me a chance, son. I won't disappoint you this time."

Nixon swallowed hard enough for Jade to see his neck maneuver. He blinked and nodded at Nick. Jade thought he might cry right there.

Jade and Nixon hung out with his parents for a little

while longer before heading to Long Island to meet her parents. The closer they got to her parents' estate the more her stomach fluttered.

Jade took his hand when they exited the car. She squeezed it just before letting it go so she could get her keys to open the door.

"Hello," she called out. "We're here." Adrenaline coursed through her. Jade felt her heartbeat at every pulse point. She walked through the large home toward the formal dining room.

So far the day had gone well—amazing, actually. Her heart was still tender from the bonding she'd just experienced between Nixon and his dad. Even the timing was perfect. Nixon's mother's early dinner gave them enough time to start out with his family and get to hers before dinner was completely over.

"Hey!" she called out over the noise in the dining room. Jade's parents, grandparents, siblings and their significant others sat around a huge table topped with a feast comprised of every signature Thanksgiving dish imaginable.

Granddad slapped his knee and cackled. His sharp laugh reached Jade's heart, making her smile without even knowing why she did. No wonder they couldn't hear her enter the house.

"Hello!" Jade waved as if she were signaling someone a block away. "We're here."

"Oh! Hey! Baby girl," Bobby Dale said, wiping his mouth with the linen napkin. He stood. El stood along with him, compelling everyone else to their feet. Bobby Dale walked over to Jade and hugged her. She snuggled in his warm embrace. Bobby Dale kissed her forehead. "Now move aside," he said, and the place fell so quiet you could hear cotton land on carpet. Bobby Dale lifted his chin and looked Nixon over. He studied him for several moments while Jade's heart selected a quicker tempo.

"Sir," Nixon said respectfully. He held out his hand. "It's a pleasure to meet you."

"Um-hmm." Bobby Dale studied him for a moment longer. "You're the fellow from Wakeman, huh?" He still hadn't touched Nixon's outstretched hand.

"Yes, sir. I'm in business development." Nixon returned his hand to his side.

"The company that tried to take us over."

Nixon took a breath. "Yes, sir."

"Uh-huh." Bobby Dale shifted on his feet and closed his arms over his chest. "And you say you like my daughter?"

"No, sir." There was a collective gasp. Bobby Dale's brows furrowed. Jade's quick-beating heart seemed to pause. "I don't *like* your daughter. I love her."

Jade's heart swelled inside her chest and found its rhythm.

El's back straightened, as if it could become stiffer.

"Mmm," Chloe and Jewel moaned in unison.

"Ha!" Jade's brother's laugh pierced the air.

"Is that so?"

"Yes. Sir."

Bobby Dale looked at him another moment before he stretched out his hand. Nixon reached forward and the men finally shook. "It's a good thing I already looked you up. I admire your business sense, young man. Seems they really like you over at Wakeman. I could like you, too. Just remember, Chandler Foods is not for sale! Ha!" Bobby Dale's big laugh eased the tension from the entire room. He patted Nixon's back. "Welcome to our home. We're glad to have you for Thanksgiving dinner."

Next, El stepped up. Chin lifted, she studied Nixon, as well. "Hello."

Nixon nodded. "Nice to meet you, Mrs. Chandler. You have an incredible home." He respectfully looked her over. "I could tell by the decor that you have impeccable taste."

A slight smile played on El's lips. "Welcome." She headed back to her seat.

El's greeting was followed by a receiving line of the rest of the family, Chloe and Jewel greeting Nixon together.

"Nice to finally meet you, Nixon," Chloe said.

"You as well." Nixon held out his hand.

Jewel pushed his hand away. "We hug around here." She pulled Nixon in for a tight one.

"This is my husband, Donovan." Chloe presented Donovan.

"What's up, man? Nice to meet you," he said. Nixon returned the greeting and they shared a masculine embrace.

"I'm Sterling." He nodded and shook Nixon's hand. "I'm Jewel's fiancé."

"Yes!" Jewel said. "That one belongs to me!"

Nixon shook his head and smiled.

"Nice to meet you, man." Jade's brother, Chris, and Nixon shook next. He presented Serenity. "This is my fiancée, Serenity."

"It's great to meet you," she said and winked at Jade. That meant Serenity approved.

Taking Nixon by the hand, Jade walked him over to her grandparents. "These are my grandparents, Eddie and Mary Kate Chandler."

"Pleasure to meet you, young man," Jade's grandfather

said, shaking Nixon's hand. "And where's my hug, young lady? Grandpa Eddie needs his smooches."

Jade hugged both her grandparents.

"Ma'am." Nixon greeted Mary Kate.

"Treat my baby girl right, you hear?" Grandma Mary Kate warned. She looked at Jade and winked. "He's cute."

"Hey! I'm sitting right here, woman," her grandfather said, pretending to be offended.

"Don't worry—you're cute, too." Grandma Mary Kate pinched his cheek before planting a kiss there.

Laughter rang out around the room. Jade and Nixon took their seats at the table and fell right into the festivities. After dessert, the men headed to the den for sports and boys talk, and the ladies hung out, sipping wine in one of the other sitting rooms. Every now and then Jade would find a reason to remove herself from the ladies' presence, just to peek in on Nixon. Each time she found him holding his own. The last time, Nixon jutted his chin forward, waved her off and winked as if to say "I'm fine." Jade smiled. The sight of Nixon laughing, sipping scotch and hanging out with the men in her family filled her heart. He'd managed to fit right in.

Chapter 32

Nixon had tried to get Jade on the phone several times during the day. He knew she was busy preparing for the foundation's annual charity ball, but he just needed to hear her voice. In the weeks since Thanksgiving, work had become overwhelming for both of them. To steal small pockets of time together, they took turns sleeping at each other's house, but by the time they got in, all they had the strength to do was cuddle and fall asleep. The next morning they started all over again.

Nixon knew Jade was busy, but he just needed a few minutes to make sure she was okay.

"How's it going?"

"Absolutely crazy!" Jade said. He could hear that admiration for her work even in her frustration.

"Let me know if there's anything I can do?"

"Aw, thanks. We're fine. Just super busy."

"Okay. I'll see you later."

"Muah!" Jade smacked a big kiss through the phone.

Next, Nixon jumped on the phone with Jade's brother, Chris. The two of them had made fast friends on Thanksgiving and spoken a few times since then. Nixon had stopped by the wine bar a few times and enjoyed Chris and his friends' jazz sessions. Being fairly new to Long Island, Nixon hadn't really made many friends there. Until Jade came along, work took up most of his time. Growing up as an only child, he didn't mind being a bit of a loner, and the few friends from his childhood now lived in other states.

Nixon also received from Chris the insight he needed to make sure he kept Jade happy. He found Jewel hilarious and Chloe was like the big sister he'd never had. Nixon both admired the Chandlers and in a short time had become quite fond of all of them, even El, who still said the least to him. Nixon enjoyed the feel of their large family, something he hadn't experienced growing up.

Trying his best to get out of the office in good time, Nixon shut down his computer and headed to the car. There was more to do. There was always more to do, but tonight was going to be special and work would have to wait. He raced home, toying with the speed limits, showered, dressed and headed to New Rochelle to get his mother.

Gloria was ready, careful not to make him wait on her. When he pulled up, she came right out, wrapped in a full-length mink to ward off the brisk December weather. Traffic heading back to The Beckingham, the exclusive Long Island country club, was as thick as Nixon anticipated. But he was still on track to get to the ball on time.

They arrived right in the middle of the cocktail hour. Jade rushed to him, kissed him, hugged his mother and was almost immediately pulled away by another guest.

Nixon tried not to let the stunning sight of Jade affect his intimate places. She looked spectacular in her red ball gown, which settled just below her smooth brown shoulders and hugged every perfectly placed curve. He imagined kissing those shoulders later, while she was still in the dress. The gown covered her shoes, but he was sure they were stylish. Her hair was swept into a polished bun and diamonds dangled from her ears.

Nixon enjoyed watching Jade and her family work the room. He smiled proudly as she floated through the ornate catering hall, greeting guest after guest, seeming to make everyone she encountered feel welcomed with her winning smile. He and his mother bet on a few of the silent-auction items before taking seats. He'd bet on the Knicks tickets because his dad was a huge fan. Nick Sr. was committed to this second chance. They spoke more regularly and Nixon thought it would be nice to spend time with him at a game, since both of them loved sports.

Nixon went to the bar and returned with two glasses of wine.

"Thank you, sweetheart," Gloria said, taking one of the glasses from him. "This place is incredible. Not like our cute little spots in New Rochelle."

"You should see Jade's parents' estate. We could put all the homes we own on that one property."

"Wow! Are you okay with all of this?" Gloria made a circle with her index finger, referring to the evident affluence of Jade's life.

"The only thing that matters to me is Jade's heart. I can hold my own."

"That's my son!" Gloria winked and patted his hand.

Jade's family's wealth was the least of Nixon's concerns. Just then, he looked up to find Jade across the room, speaking with a guest but peeking his way. She acknowledged him with a small wave and a smile before focusing back on her guest.

A distinguished-looking gentleman played a few notes on a small xylophone and guests began to make their way into the spacious main ballroom. It wasn't until they'd gotten inside that Nixon realized the massive number of people in attendance. Now he understood why the family hadn't held the ball at their venue by the pier. As large as Chandler's was, it was too intimate to accommodate a crowd of this magnitude. And the caliber of guests was impressive. Nixon noted the presence of elected officials, prominent businessmen who had graced the covers of the business magazines he read, and a few famed Long Island residents. Nick Sr. managed to make it right as the program was starting.

As the cochairs of the Chandler Foundation's board, El and Chris took to the podium to welcome their guests and thank their sponsors. They directed everyone's attention to the several television screens around the room to watch a video of testimonials from the organizations that the foundation supported. Next a few young people from Serenity's music program played a beautiful rendition of "The Wind beneath My Wings."

As wonderful as the program was, Nixon couldn't wait for it to be over. He had something for Jade after this was done. Watching her grace and brilliance in action filled him not only with admiration, but desire, as well. Nixon became as anxious as a child anticipating Christmas Day. He suffered through the remainder of the festivities until the only people left behind were the family and their staff.

"Come with me." He took Jade by the hand.

"But we're not finished wrapping up here."

"I'll bring you back," Nixon said and kissed her lips, swallowing her next attempt at protesting.

"Oh!" Jade touched her lips. She smiled and then shimmied. "Okay. Where are you taking me, Mr. Gaines? Are you being naughty?"

Nixon paused, shooting a piercing look directly into her eyes. Jade squealed and giggled. She looked behind her as if to see who might be watching them slip out, then practically skipped alongside Nixon.

Heading past the winding staircase, Nixon led Jade out on the terrace and down a lush, lit path bordered with winter greenery. He removed his tuxedo jacket and tossed it over her shoulders.

"Woo! Where are we going?"

Nixon looked back at her and winked. She followed him a few more feet. A line of tall evergreens blocked their line of sight.

"Close your eyes."

"Nixon!" she sang. "What are you up to?" But Jade followed his instructions, squeezing his hand tighter and holding on to his arm to keep her footing.

Nixon reached his destination—the garden gazebo. He guided Jade up the few steps onto the structure and said, "Open your eyes."

When she did, Jade gasped and covered her mouth. Nixon was on one knee, holding a stunning diamond that gleamed in the moonlight. Nick Sr. stood near Mr. Chandler, while Gloria stood next to El. The rest of the family had positioned themselves around the perimeter of the gazebo, surrounding them. Jade looked around and tears filled her eyes.

"Yes! Nixon. Oh my goodness. Yes. I'll marry you."

"Girl!" Jewel said. "He didn't even ask you yet."

Their families' laughter mixed beautifully together.

Nixon imagined the joy of the sounds they would create together for years to come.

Jade's giggles fluttered through the night air. Nixon held her hand and gazed into her eyes. "Jade Chandler." Nixon thought back to the first day he had laid eyes on Jade, remembered the way she'd made him shiver with just a passing touch. He could feel the tingle from the charge that still passed between them in their caresses. His heart seemed to double in size at that very moment. "Will you make me the happiest man in the world and be my wife?"

"Yes!" Jade bounced up and down on her toes.

Nixon had to steady her hand to get the ring on. She took him by the lapels of his tux, dragged him to his feet and threw her arms around his neck. He kissed her lips and couldn't seem to get enough. Capturing her tongue in a sensual dance, he didn't want to let her go. Just that quickly, Nixon had forgotten about their families surrounding them, until they teased the newly engaged couple with a collection of whoops, oohs and aahs. Finally, he released her lips, picked her up and spun her around.

"Woo-o!" Jade shouted, holding up her left hand to show off her ring.

Nixon let Jade down, her body sliding along the front of his.

She looked into his eyes. "You've made me the happiest woman in the world."

* * * * *